1.15

First they used drugs to severely impair agent N3's mind and body—then they dumped him into a black void . . .

"Before my cigarette lighter died out I took a look around and could see nothing at all. There were no walls or obstacles on the floor. I felt much the same as an ant dropped in the middle of the Sahara desert. Somewhere there must be an end to all this nothingness, a wall, a person, a piece of machinery. Anything to tell me that I was not all alone here; best of all, there must be a way out of here, some contact with civilization."

NICK CARTER IS IT!

‘‘Nick Carter out-Bonds James Bond.’’

–Buffalo Evening News

‘‘Nick Carter is America’s #1 espionage agent.’’

–Variety

Nick Carter is razor-sharp suspense.’’

–King Featurs

‘‘Nick Carter is extraordinarily big.’’

–Bestsellers

‘‘Nick Carter has attracted an army of addicted readers . . . the books are fast, have plenty of action and just the right degree of sex . . . Nick Carter is the American James Bond, suave, sophisticated, a killer with both the ladies and the enemy.’’

–The New York Times

FROM THE NICK CARTER
KILLMASTER SERIES

AND THE NEXT THE KING
CHECKMATE IN RIO
THE COYOTE CONNECTION
THE DAY OF THE DINGO
DEATH MISSION: HAVANA
DOOMSDAY SPORE
EIGHTH CARD STUD
THE GALLAGHER PLOT
THE JUDAS SPY
KATMANDU CONTRACT
THE MAN WHO SOLD DEATH
THE NICHOVEV PLOT
THE OUSTER CONSPIRACY
THE PAMPLONA AFFAIR
THE PEMES CHART
THE Q MAN
THE REDOLMO AFFAIR
THE SATAN TRAP
THE SIGN OF THE PRAYER SHAWL
SIX BLOODY SUMMER DAYS
SOCIETY OF NINE
STRIKE OF THE HAWK
SUICIDE SEAT
TARANTULA STRIKE
TEMPLE OF FEAR
TEN TIMES DYNAMITE
THUNDERSTRIKE IN SYRIA
TIME CLOCK OF DEATH
TRIPLE CROSS
TURKISH BLOODBATH
UNDER THE WALL
WAR FROM THE CLOUDS
THE WEAPON OF NIGHT

Dedicated to the men of the
Secret Services of the
United States of America

THE GOLDEN BULL

A DIVISION OF CHARTER COMMUNICATIONS INC.
A GROSSET & DUNLAP COMPANY

THE GOLDEN BULL

A Charter Original.

First Charter Printing June 1981
Published simultaneously in Canada
Manufactured in the United States of America

2 4 6 8 0 9 7 5 3 1

THE GOLDEN BULL

ONE

I wasn't in the best of moods when I arrived at Dupont Circle in Washington, D.C. I had been in the midst of preparing a steak and champagne dinner as a prelude to seducing Natalie when Hawk's call had come through. I had had to bundle Natalie unceremoniously out of my apartment, then face the cold, drizzling rain that so often prevails in our nation's capital. As always happens on cold, rainy nights, cabs were next to impossible to find and I could feel the time slipping away. Not that Hwak had said anything about urgency, but I knew him well enough to know that he would not have summoned me to his office at 8:30 on a Saturday evening if it were not urgent.

I finally reached Amalgamated Press and Wire Service, which was the cover name for AXE headquarters, and had to go through the same identification routine, with the same guard, that I had been through so many times before. He was a wiry little guy who looked to be closer to sixty than fifty; with the loose coveralls he wore and the shambling gait he affected, he looked a typical run-of-the-mill janitor. I knew him well enough, though, to know that he held a fifth degree black belt in judo and that beneath his loose coveralls he carried a cocked Smith and Wesson .38 revolver.

"Dirty night, Mr. Carter," he said, after we were through with the formalities. "You'd better go straight up. Mr. Hawk's waiting for you."

I ran up the stairs, tapped on Hawk's door and let myself in. The moment I stepped into his office I could see how worried he was. Hawk normally was seated at his desk with his face buried in a pile of paperwork when I arrived. Tonight he was pacing up and down, worrying the end of an unlighted cigar much as a terrier might gnaw the end of a bone.

I slipped into a chair by the desk and waited for him to acknowledge the fact that I had answered his summons. It took a little while. He continued to pace up and down for a full two minutes before he turned to me and scowled.

"You took your time getting here."

"I'm sorry, sir," I said. "I got here as quickly as I could. You know how difficult it is to get a cab on a rainy night in Washington."

Hawk just grunted and continued his pacing. Three more traversals of the room and he stopped, aiming that dead cigar at me as though it were a lethal weapon.

"Gold, Nick. What do you know about gold?"

"The basics, sir. I know of course that it's a precious metal and that it's the basis for the currency of most countries in the world. I know that its purity is rated commercially in karats—the higher the rating, the soft-ter it is and the less practical for ornamental jewelry purposes. I also know that over the past few years it has taken some tremendous jumps on the world market and that within the last few years the government passed a law permitting private citizens to buy and own gold."

"What about you, Nick? Have you been buying any gold?"

It was a ridiculous question and coming from anybody else I would have treated it as such, but David Hawk wasn't in the habit of asking ridiculous questions.

"No, sir. Investments of any kind are an insurance against old age. I don't expect to live long enough to be able to make use of them."

He grunted again. "A lot of people do."

"Most people aren't in our business," I said.

"That's right. Most people have turned to gold as an investment, because as long as the price keeps going up, their investment will grow. Even if the market goes down, they will still have a healthy capital sum. It cannot disappear like it did in so many cases back in the big crash of twenty-nine."

I looked at the frown on his face. "Is that bad, sir?" I asked.

"Investing money in gold keeps it off the market. It keeps it out of the savings-and-loan people's hands so that there is less money available for housing and mortgages, so that our economy hurts."

It wasn't like Hawk to summon me to his office for a lecture on economics, and I felt that he was talking as much to himself as he was to me. I waited.

"Gold," he went on, "unlike so many other commodities can be completely untraceable. Melt it down into a bar or an ingot and you can sell it anywhere in the world. As long as we have the same amount of it floating around the world, it's going to stay at a fairly stable rate. But start unleashing vast quantities of it through a black market and the price will plummet. Not only has the housing market been affected, but all the little investors have suddenly lost much of their capital."

My curiosity finally got the better of me. "How does all of this affect AXE, sir?" I asked.

"Under normal circumstances," he told me, "it wouldn't. Somebody has been smuggling gold into the United States in such quantities that the Treasury Department asked me to lend them a man to help stop it."

I was a little dismayed. "I see," I said. "Then you want me to give the Treasury people a hand for a while."

"Not quite, Nick," he told me quietly. "I lent them a man, N17; a little inexperienced perhaps, but a good man nonetheless."

"Then were do I come in, sir?"

"Just four hours ago, N17 was found in a back alley in Tijuana. His throat had been slit."

I said, "I'm very sorry to hear that, sir." I meant it. N17 was a quiet, yet enthusiastic young man named Dennis Gordon, with whom I had worked just once. I had liked him and was genuinely sorry to hear that he had bought it so early in the game.

Hawk scowled and clamped down on his cigar again. "You know how I feel about my people, Nick. That's why I'm putting you on the case."

"Do we have any leads, sir?"

"N17 was on loan to the Treasury people. He made all his reports to them. They will be able to fill you in. That's what's so frustrating; I know nothing at all of what has been going on. In time of course I shall get it all from the Treasury people, but I think we need to get after it as soon as possible."

"Contacts, sir?"

"The T-man in Tijuana is Paul Winters. As far as he's concerned you're replacing N17. However, I want full reports on your progress and I shall expect you to use your own judgment as to where you go and what you do."

"In other words," I said, "I remain fully responsible to you, but I am to give the impression that I am working strictly under the orders of the Treasury Department."

"Precisely."

"You suspect more than gold smuggling, then?"

"Nick, the operatives of AXE, as you know, are the most highly trained of this or any other country. N17 may have been less experienced than many of my operatives but that didn't make him any less efficient. It's unthinkable that any AXE agent could get his throat cut in the back alley of some border town unless he was lured there for that purpose."

I nodded. "Do you think that it may have been done by the executive branch of the KGB?"

"Certainly by the executive branch of some nation's secret police. Nobody else would be good enough. I've got a hunch about this one, Nick," Hawk said more seriously. "The gold smuggling is big—very big. It has the Treasury people very worried, but somehow I get the feeling that there's a lot more to it than just that. I think the gold smuggling is just the tip of the iceberg. Get down there right away, contact Winters and see if you can find out what's going on."

I stood up. "Very well, sir."

"And for heaven's sake," said Hawk leveling that dead cigar at me again, "let me know what's happening."

When our B747 landed in San Diego the next morning the weather was much more pleasant than it had been in Washington. I rented a car and made the short drive to the border crossing, and on into Tijuana. I stopped at the first pay phone I came to, called the Hotel Bahia and asked for Paul Winters. As soon as I identified myself he told me to come straight over.

Winters was a tall, lean man with close-cropped hair who looked and sounded like efficiency personified. He shook hands with a firm, dry clasp and poured me a cup of coffee.

"I've heard of you, Carter. Seems like you have quite a reputation."

"I do my best," I told him.

"Don't we all?" he muttered half to himself.

"What's the story?" I asked. "Can you tell me what Dennis Gordon was up to when he was killed?"

"I don't know much about it, but then nobody does. The basic situation is this. There is a fantastic amount of gold going into the United States and being sold on the black market at about four hundred and fifty dollars an ounce."

I whistled. "I thought the price was closer to seven hundred."

"It is," he told me, "legally anyway. So with unlimited supplies coming in to sell at that price, you can imagine what's going to happen to our economy."

"Somebody must be losing their shirt on that deal," I said. "Or else it's been stolen. Have there been any reports of stolen shipments of bullion?"

"None at all. Not from anywhere in the world."

"Then it seems to me that either somebody is keeping very quiet about the loss of an enormous amount of gold—which doesn't make sense unless they had acquired it illegally—or else somebody is going to great expense to undermine the economy of the United States."

"You're right of course. And this is the problem that we've been battling with since it first came to our attention about a month ago."

I pushed my coffee cup toward him for a refill and snapped a light to one of my gold monogrammed cigarettes. "What about Gordon?"

"The only lead we've had in this case was an anonymous phone call telling us that the gold was coming from South America through Mexico under the guise of legitimate exports. We went through a list of people big enough to be able to handle gold shipments of that size. We split the list four ways and Gordon got three names to check out. He called me two days ago from Mexico City to say that the first two names on the list appeared to be on the level and that he was going to work on the third one."

"Then you think he may have stumbled onto something with this third person and found out more than was healthy for him?"

"No," said Winters. "As a matter of fact, I don't. The third person on that list was Tina Rodriguez, one of the wealthiest women in South America. She owns copper, tin and lead mines all over the continent, and a variety of businesses. One of them manufactures and exports souvenir items; the biggest seller is a bull cast in lead and painted gold."

"That sounds ideal," I told him. "Make every third or fourth one out of pure gold and the chances are they'd get through customs every time."

"Do you think we hadn't thought of that?" he asked bitterly. "I had every shipment stopped at the border for three solid weeks, and every damned souvenir casting inspected."

"And?"

"Everyone was lead. I expected to find at least one lousy little bull in pure gold. But no, not one; and we ruined every item in every shipment just checking them. Now my boss is mad at me because Tina Rodriguez has filed suit for compensation in the full amount of the value of every shipment."

"Perhaps she was tipped off," I said, "and sent through innocent shipments."

"No way. The first two shipments were already on the way before we got the tip off; it would have been impossible to have switched them."

He reached into a drawer of the dressing table behind him and handed me what had once been the figure of a bull with lowered head and pawing hoof. I say what had been, because the figure was scarred with more than a dozen knife slashes, and in each cut was the silver gray of lead. I hefted it in my hand. It wasn't light.

"How many of these in one shipment?" I asked.

"Two thousand."

"This thing weighs about a pound, so that if one in every ten were cast in gold there'd be two hundred pounds of pure gold in every shipment. That's thirty-two hundred ounces. Even at black market prices of four hundred and fifty dollars an ounce, that comes out to almost twenty-four-and-a-half million dollars per shipment."

"My thinking exactly. That's why I had to have everyone of them checked. And they all look exactly like the one in your hand."

I shrugged. "Do you have any other ideas?"

"I do, as a matter of fact. I think that during his conversation with Tina Rodriguez, or one of her business associates, Gordon stumbled onto something that made him suspicious of one of the people he had already dismissed as innocent. I think he rushed back here to check something out and somebody got wise to him."

It was entirely possible of course, but then it was just as possible that he had come across something that had international ramifications. Dennis Gordon was, after all, an AXE operative. Whatever it was he had discovered may have had nothing at all to do with gold smuggling. But whether it was or not, it was enough to get him killed, and it was my job to find out who and why.

"Can I see his body?" I asked.

"I don't see why not. We have a pretty good working arrangement with the Mexican police. But what do you expect to find out?"

"I won't know until I've seen it," I told him. "After that, I think I'd better go and see Tina Rodriguez and try to find out what it was it was that sent Gordon rushing back here."

TWO

Dennis Gordon was not a wholesome sight. In Mexico's climate a corpse doesn't last long, and there had been no attempt to pretty up the remains. He had been attacked from behind with a stiletto, probably not unlike Hugo, the ten-inch blade I wear in a sheath strapped to the inside of my right forearm. Whoever had attacked him had pushed the blade into the side of his neck then thrust it forward, tearing his entire throat out with the blade so that he would avoid the gush of blood.

Death was perhaps not instantaneous, but he could not have lain there long before he succumbed to the loss of blood. His face and extremities had the white, wax-like texture that indicated severe loss of blood. I signed the papers making the identification official, went through his belongings and had them sent on to AXE headquarters in Washington, then went back to see Winters.

He seemed not to have moved very much since I had left him. He still had a cup of coffee in front of him and was gnawing at a stub of pencil apparently looking for inspiration to write his daily report on the arrival of the new boy. I pulled up a chair and helped myself to coffee.

''Nothing much to be learned there,'' I commented.

He looked at me with an I-told-you-so look.

''It was done by an expert,'' I continued, ''from behind so that he would not get splattered by the blood. Nothing will draw attention faster than running down the street covered with blood from head to foot—even in Tijuana.''

Winters nodded briefly and turned his attention back to his report. ''Where do I find this Tina Rodriguez person?'' I asked.

''Normally, when she is in Central America she lives at her villa in Mexico CIty, but Gordon said someething about her going to the Majestic Hotel in Acapulco. The way she lives it shouldn't be hard to track her down.''

I drove back to San Diego and booked a flight to Acapulco. I wanted it to appear as though I arrived directly from the States without having stopped in Tijuana, which could cause suspicion among certain people whose attention I would prefer to avoid.

It was a very short flight, but a very luxurious one; I suppose the destination being the hub of the tourist attraction had a lot to do with the quality of the personal services. As I sipped on the complimentary champagne I thought about Tina Rodriguez, reported to be one of the wealthiest women in South America, and decided my approach would be that of the jet-set playboy—the type who has more money than sense. If the Rodriguez woman had any taste at all she would be bored by these parasitic hangers-on, but at least it would give me a chance to get close to her.

I took a cab to the Majestic Hotel making sure that I overtipped the driver to create the right image. When the desk clerk came out I asked for the hotel's best suite, half expecting to be told that Tina Rodriguez was already occupying it. The desk clerk hit the bell push and gave a key to the bellhop. As I followed him I turned back to the desk clerk as though on an afterthought.

"Is Tina Rodriguez registered here?"

"Mrs. Rodriguez," I was told coldly, "keeps a permanent suite here. I don't know if she is in residence at this particular time. Her secretary is always here. I suggest you direct your inquiries to her."

I tracked after the bellhop to the elevator and on up to the top floor where I was shown a sumptuous suite. I tipped him lavishly which was a pretty good deal for him since all he had had to carry was my room key.

There was a small entrance hall opening off from the main door which led to the large living room. I wandered around savoring the plush elegance of the three bathrooms with connecting bedrooms. I built myself a small gin and tonic at the inconspicuous bar in the living room, stripped and immersed myself in the nearest sunken tub where I made like a Roman emperor.

After the tub I made a dash across the room for a cold shower trying to figure why it was that I didn't get lost in all that empty space. Back in the living room with the second gin and tonic and a cigarette, I put my feet on the cocktail table and admired the flawless copies of Monet and Cezanne that adorned the walls.

My stomach and my watch told me that it was dinner time, and I found a clean shirt and a pair of my less disreputable jeans and went down to the dining room where I found a seat at a table with my back to the wall. It was an off night for the tourists and the dining room was only about half full. I ordered the New York steak with all the trimmings and a half bottle of chilled rosé wine and settled back to watch the crowd.

For a while the crowd seemed to consist mainly of off-season tourists with a few honeymoon couples. Then about halfway through my dinner a group of five people came in. There was a raven-haired beauty, a peroxide blonde and what was obviously three beach bums, long on the muscle and short on the equipment normally stored between the ears. The women were bejeweled far in excess of what their escorts could have afforded. I looked over the three men again. This time one of them appeared to have the air of a successful businessman, but I stood my first appraisal of the other two as beach bums. Take away their Brooks Brothers suits and I doubted that they would have been able to make change for a quarter.

The group had apparently been drinking steadily all day because none of them was felling any pain. Just after they started dinner a mariachi band came in and started to do their stuff. Both women got up to dance and my previous impression of their drinking habits was confirmed. All four of them were having considerable trouble maintaining their balance. When they sat down again it was all too apparent that it was the women who were giving the orders. When the waiter brought the check he handed it to the man I had identified as a businessman; he signed it after scrutinizing it carefully.

I sat there nursing a cup of coffee and had just about decided that there was not much point in sticking around the dining room and dance floor when a shadow fell across me. I looked up and saw one of the beach bums looking down on me from behind his suntan. He was over six feet tall and his shoulders in the white tuxedo appeared to be every bit of four feet wide. I looked him up and down coldly.

"Anything I can do for you?" I asked.

"Not personally," he told me with a leer. "There's a lady across the way who wants to dance with you. I'm just the bearer of the glad tidings."

I said, "You are also the bearer of about half a pint of cheap cologne, or do you always smell like a whorehouse? My respects to the lady in question, but my reason for being here is to eat a quiet dinner, not to see what or who I could pick up."

He didn't like that much, but I wasn't there to win any popularity contest. He flexed his muscles under the padding of the tuxedo and dropped a hand on my shoulder with a grip that was intended to make my eyes water. "Do you know who you're talking to, punk?"

"From the smell of you, I'd say the chief honcho at the local pox clinic. Now get your hand off me before I break something, like your head.

He tightened his grip on my shoulder and started to lift me out of my chair. I came up with him until I was almost at my full height, then I reached up, took the middle three fingers of his hand and bent them all the way back.

That doesn't sound like much, but it can be excruciatingly painful and any resistance will lead to dislocated fingers. "Just tell the lady, thanks, but no thanks, not even if she smells as pretty as you do." I turned him around and pushed him gently in the direction of his party.

I watched him walk back to the rest of his party where he talked animatedly while nursing his sore fingers. He seemed not to be getting much sympathy unless it was from me. When it was apparent that no further emissary was to be dispatched to collect me, I paid my bill and went up to my suite where I got a good night's dream-free sleep.

I was awake early the next morning and called for orange juice and coffee before I went down to the pool for a few quick laps to stimulate my circulation. Coming out of the pool I stretched out on one of the mattress pads to soak up some of the early morning sunshine before I started my day's work. My plan was to make the acquaintance of Tina Rodriguez to develop a rapport with her to find out what I could about the gold situation. It was not yet eight o'clock, far too early for an elderly lady to be up and about so I resigned myself to making the most of my surroundings.

Lying there I let my mind wander until a large glass came into my view. The glass was held by a hand, and I let my eyes follow the arm until it came to a well-filled bikini top. Nothing will wake a man up so fast as a sight such as this. It has the same effect on me as a carrot on a stubborn mule. I sat up taking note of the equally well-filled lower half of the bikini.

"Here, drink this and see if it will put you in a better mood."

I said, "My moods are always dependent on my surroundings, and from here the scenery couldn't be improved upon."

"Then why did you insult me last night?"

I managed to tear my eyes away from the bikini and found myself face to face with the brunette I had last seen in the dining room the previous evening. "Me? Insult you? Never."

"Then why wouldn't you dance with me?"

"Was that you? I didn't like your messenger; or to be precise I didn't like his perfume, and he seemed to have his own ideas of imposing his will on others."

"He's just an impetuous boy with a handful of sore fingers. What did you do to him, for Pete's sake?"

"I bent his finger. He was lucky I was in a good mood or I might have broken his head."

"I don't think you're in any better mood this morning. You'd better drink this."

"What is it?" I looked suspiciously at the amber fluid.

"It's a mood rejuvenator. Guaranteed to make crabby old men fit to socialize with."

"What's in it?"

"My usual morning pick-me-up. Champagne and orange juice."

"Sounds good. But if I drink it you'll have to promise to keep your sweet-smelling errand boy out of my hair. I'm a very reasonable man, but I can do without a lot of cheap perfume."

"Oh, Al's all right. He does what he's paid to do."

"Which is?"

"Run errands, provide escort service, drive a car."

"You must have quite a retinue."

"Doesn't everybody?"

"Maybe I'm different, but I prefer my own company."

I reached for my cigarette case and offered her one. She took one and tapped it on her thumbnail then looked intently at the initials I have embossed on the filter.

"What does N.C. stand for?"

"Nick Cramer. And yours?"

"You already know my name."

"What makes you think that?"

"The first thing you did when you arrived yesterday was to sign the register and then ask if I was here."

"You mean you're Tina Rodriguez."

"You seem to have a penchant for insulting people."

"Not intentionally. I'm just surprised. I expected a much older woman."

"Nobody said I had to be Alvin Rodriguez's first wife. I married him after he had made his fortune, while he still had a taste for a girlish figure."

"I admire his taste."

"It was a pretty good marriage. I was able to take an interest in his business affairs unlike so many social-climbing women one meets in Peru. The last few weeks of his life I ran the entire corporation. He died knowing that it was in good hands."

I allowed my eyes to roam over the bikini. "I find it difficult to picture you sitting behind a desk running a conglomerate."

"I don't do that any more. I've proved myself. Now I have a business manager. The man who was at dinner with me last night."

"The one who didn't look like a beach bum?"

"Curtis McBride. He's my executive vice president."

She helped herself to another of my cigarettes and leaned forward to my light. "When I was running the corporation for Alvin I formed a habit of working twelve hours a day and sleeping only four hours a night. The people who travel with me have to have their eight hours of sleep a night which gives me a couple of hours in the early morning all to myself. I hate like hell to waste it; let's go swimming."

I bounded to my feet and led the way to the pool where I followed her perfect jackknife into the cool blue waters. She was an excellent swimmer with the effortless grace of the natural athlete. We romped in the pool for a while until it started to get crowded with the rest of the hotel's guests, then we climbed out and claimed a poolside table where I ordered breakfast to be served after a fresh pitcher of champagne and orange juice.

By the time we had finished breakfast the area surrounding the pool was beginning to take on all the characteristics of the New York subway on a Friday evening. "Let's go find some deserted beach," I suggested. "I'll have the hotel make us up a picnic lunch. I'm sure there must be some place in Acapulco less crowded than this."

"Sounds good," she told me, "but I have a meeting with my Mexican tax attorneys at eleven. How about dinner tonight?"

"On condition you leave the muscle-bound beach bums behind. We can find a good restaurant somewhere around town; I'll pick you up at seven. Where are you?"

"Penthouse D, and I'll call off the hangers-on."

She left me then, weaving her way between the sprawling tourists to find her suite to get dressed for the meeting with her attorneys. I lit another cigarette, but the press of the crowd was a little too much for me so I went up to my suite to shower and get dressed to make an appearance downtown. Before I left I encoded a telegram to Hawk telling him that I had made contact with the prime suspect. I dictated the telegram over the phone and then climbed into a pair of jeans and an old sports shirt for a trip to town. When I returned to my penthouse, I was the proud possessor of a lightweight tuxedo with all the fashionable accessories.

At seven o'clock the door to Penthouse D was opened by my aromatic acquaintance of the previous evening who stood aside to let me in and then spent the rest of his time glaring at me. Under any other circumstances I would have goaded him into starting something, but I didn't want to jeopardize the tenuous foothold I had on Tina Rodriguez's acquaintance. I was handed a glass of champagne and introduced to the peroxide blonde with the most unlikely name of Gonsalez, Curtis McBride, the executive vice president of the Rodriguez conglomerate, and the other beach bum, Willie Chan, whose name indicated a youth spent in the Hawaiian islands.

There was very little conversation, I suspect because Tina was in the habit of surrounding herself with "yes men," while for my part I had little interest in engaging that type of person in intimate conversation. Al was dispatched to round up the limousine and chauffeur and the conversation came to a grinding halt. When he returned with the news that the car was waiting at the main entrance for us, we left with Tina clinging to my arm like some wifely appendage.

I have been in Acapulco many times but the restaurant scene can change overnight with places going out of business, others starting up and shifts of management, not to mention the unceasing flow of chefs from one establishment to the next. When we climbed into the back seat of the Rolls Royce, I beckoned the doorman over and asked him to give the driver directions to the best restaurant in town. This was not only in keeping with my playboy image but gave the impression that I was a stranger in town and that our date had been the outcome of a casual meeting. I was still concerned about my indiscreet inquiry at the registration desk as to Tina's whereabouts. If I was asked I could say that I had been asked to look her up by some fictitious maiden aunt in Washington. The upper social circle is a very tight-knit group—but I had no doubt that I could bluff my way through it, if I was asked. Tina had apparently forgotten about it, however, and I was content to let it lie.

The driver took us to a large place overlooking the ocean with a Polynesian decor and a menu one third of which was American food, one third Mexican and one third Polynesian with a band of wandering musicians wending their way among the tables.

We drank scorpions, feasted on lobster and danced under the stars then drove back to the hotel with a cold bottle of champagne taken from the bar in the back of the car. By the time we got back to the hotel the champagne bottle was empty and we left it in the car along with the glasses for the chauffeur to clean up. We walked through the foyer and rode the elevator up to the top floor.

When we got out of the elevator Tina turned to the right and started walking along the passage. I grabbed her arm. "Hey, where do you think you're going? You live that way," and I pointed over my shoulder.

"I'm not going to my suite. We're going to yours. There're too many people in my place. I can't even pace the floor without tripping over somebody's feet."

I unlocked the door and watched her scurrying through the suite. "Nick, what do you do with all this room?"

"The best furnishings always go with the best suite," I told her, "and I'm a man who likes the best of everything. I admit I can't use more than one bathroom at a time, or sleep in more than one bed, but it's nice to know that they're available."

"Have you got any champagne?"

"I expect so. If they haven't stocked my bar completely, I'll move out in the morning." I found a bottle of Dom Perignon in the refrigerator, popped the cork and filled two glasses.

"Now you can show me around."

"I thought you'd looked around."

She slipped an arm through mine. "But I want you to show me your favorite bedroom."

"That's easy. My favorite bedroom is whichever one you happen to be in."

"Talk, talk, talk, is that all you do? Show me," and she led the way into the largest bedroom, the one with the king-sized bed, struggling with the straps of her evening gown.

THREE

I let Tina out of my suite in the early hours of the morning and then went back in to order a solitary breakfast, leaving her to worry about what excuses she should make to anybody who saw her coming home at that hour of the morning in an evening gown with one torn shoulder strap. She had a breakfast meeting with her tax attorneys who had apparently come up with some new government regulations to take more money from her. I have heard that the biggest problem of rich people is protecting what they have accumulated from the ever-grasping hands of the public, but nobody is so greedy as a government, no matter which one. It's a problem I have never been cursed with and I find it difficult to sympathize with anybody in that position.

We had decided to take a picnic lunch to some deserted beach that day and after breakfast I lay around the pool absorbing sunshine. This was turning out to be more of a vacation than an assignment but I didn't let my conscience bother me. The obvious thing to do was cultivate Tina's friendship to find out what I could about this gold smuggling, and if I had to laze around like a tourist to do it, then that was my good fortune.

One of the staff came over to tell me that the picnic lunch I had ordered was ready and I told him to put it in Tina's limousine. She joined me at the pool wearing a scrap of a sundress. I made polite inquiries about the outcome of her meeting with the tax people, but she seemed disinclined to discuss it at any length. After a pitcher of champagne and orange juice we climbed into the Rolls and headed for the beach.

After a gambol in the surf and a lunch consisting mainly of cold chicken and even colder champagne we lay spread out on the sand. Tina reached for the second bottle of champagne and popped the cork. I lay there listless watching the cotton puff clouds drift across the incredible blue of the sky. In the distance I could see Tina's chauffeur flicking a rag over the limousine. She handed me a glass of champagne and, as she did, I had one of my intuitive feelings that I had been brought there for some specific purpose in addition to soaking up sunshine and champagne. Her words confirmed it.

"What brings you to Acapulco, Nick?"

"The weather."

"Is that all?"

"Normally," I said. "I live in Washington which can be pretty miserable at this time of the year. Along about now I start looking for some place that's a little warmer before my blood freezes in my veins."

"I had an idea you may have been on a business trip along with the vacation."

I said, "Inherited money doesn't need to be looked

after. My grandfather took care of all that, way back when."

"Why Acapulco?"

"Just for a change. I normally spend this part of the year in the Caribbean. I have a house outside Ochos Rio in Jamaica." AXE has a house there and if anybody was going to check it they would come up against a dead end of David Hawk's making.

"How long will you be staying here?"

"Until I have a yen to be somewhere else. Why all this sudden interest in my movements?"

"I was just thinking it's about time for my annual visit to my lead mines in Uruguay after which I usually detour through Mexico to take a look at my industries. If you don't have any other plans why don't you come with me. You would be a refreshing change from the company I usually keep on these trips. And it would take care of the bad weather spell in Washington."

"When are you leaving?"

"I wound up my tax business today so there is no reason why I should not leave tomorrow unless you have something to keep you."

"I never have anything to keep me anywhere. What time suits you?"

"I'll have somebody check out the flight times. If we catch a morning flight to Mexico City we should be able to catch a through flight to Montevideo in the afternoon."

"Give me a call when you're ready to leave."

We went to dinner that night and drank more of the same champagne, danced to the same music under the same stars, then tumbled into bed to perform the same ritualistic fumblings that culminated in the same desperate poundings that men and women have performed ever since time began. Tina left early to supervise the packing of her luggage, giving me a chance to call Hawk to let him know my destination and to expect some results from my investigation of her industries. I still favored the theory that Tina Rodriguez or one of her staff was responsible for the gold smuggling,all I had to do was to figure out how they managed to get it past the border. I had not forgotten the murder of Dennis Gordon; but one would lead inevitably to the other.

It took me all of three minutes to pack. It would have taken me less, but I now had a tuxedo to drag around with me. I had toyed with the idea of giving it away to some charitable institution, but that would only leave a trail a mile wide for anybody who was interested in my movements, and from the way Tina Rodriguez lived I would probably need it in Montevideo and Mexico City and wherever else she chose to lead me. Sometimes I think that that part of progress which was responsible for the invention of the disposable razor and wash-and-wear shirts was formed with me specifically in mind. With my flight bag bulging with a tuxedo, formal shirt and pants, my spare shirt and my less disreputable jeans, a spare pair of briefs and my toothbrush I walked down to the registration desk and checked out and went up to Penthouse D where I handed the sum total of my baggage into the reluctant hands of Al.

Three minutes later we were in the Rolls Royce headed for tthe airport listening to the incessant chatter of Tina's tourist guide to Montevideo and all the reasons why I could not have possibly lived before I had seen her darling villa. We ran into a problem at the airport when we were told that there was no through flight to Montevideo that day. However, when one is as rich as Tina Rodriguez all things are possible and Curtis McBride was promptly dispatched to charter an aircraft to meet us at Mexico City for the run to Montevideo. I was starting to get used to this VIP treatment and liking it more every day.

It was early in the morning when we reached Montevideo. We took two taxis: one for myself and Tina, the other for Curtis McBride and all of Tina's luggage. There was very little to see at that time of morning, well before dawn, so I was spared the homespun tourist guide, but I was not spared the fragrant scents of frangipani, bougainvillea and the hibiscus that always assaults one's sense of smell in Montevideo. We drove into the courtyard of the villa and into the waiting arms of the permanent staff. From the way the taxi had been climbing for the past few minutes I suspected that we were on a hillside overlooking the famous harbor, but I would have to wait until daylight to make sure.

The housekeeper, a portly lady in her best dressing gown, led us into a stone-floored kitchen with a fireplace that had been built to roast a team of oxen and fed us delicacies which I thought had been made with loving care as soon as word had reached her that her mistress was in transit. And, of course, there was the ever-present bottle of champagne. I was interested to note that the champagne was Dom Perignon, thought to be the best in the world, so apparently Tina had stocked all her villas with it. Personally I'm just as happy with a bottle of beer, but if drinking champagne would allow me to become Tina's confidante and further my cause I was willing to overlook the damage to my liver.

I was ushered off to bed at the finish of our snack. I was shown a room with a king-sized bed and enough room to hold a barn dance with an adjoining bathroom that put the Majestic Hotel's ablution facilities to shame. I took a brief shower to rid myself of the day's traveling soil and slid between the cool, crisp sheets to overcome the jet lag.

I am not in the habit of sleeping deeply or for any length of time, and I have trained myself to wake at the slightest sound, but I had barely climbed into bed before I heard the door open and the pad of bare feet coming toward me. I slid my hand under the pillow and grasped the butt of Wilhelmina, my constant companion on these ventures. Wilhelmina is a vastly outdated Luger pistol firing fully metal-jacketed 9mm slugs, which when I am formally dressed I carry in a chamois shoulder holster.

I am seldom without Wilhelmina, Hugo or Pierre. Hugo is the pencil-thin stiletto I carry in a sheath strapped to my right forearm, and Pierre is the tiny globular gas bomb I wear taped to the inside of my groin. For the past few days I had, of necessity, gone about unarmed. There is no place to conceal a twenty-ounce handgun or a ten-inch stiletto when one is dressed in a swimsuit, and the romping I had been enjoying in bed with Tina would have caused some comment on my wearing Pierre, not to mention the ultimate danger of Tina's thrashing around triggering a lethal dose of toxic gas.

I felt the bed move and heard Tina's sultry whisper, "Asleep already?"

I put my left hand out and filled it with warm, soft girl. Either she had been in a terrible hurry to get home where she could do it on familiar ground, or somebody had been putting Spanish Fly in her champagne, because she wasted no time. She threw one leg over me and straddled me while guiding me into her, making little sobbing sounds as I penetrated her. When two people come together with that much impatience it doesn't last very long.

After a few thrusts I lay back while Tina went to work on me to revive the passion I had spent. Before long I was rampant and raring to go again. I pulled her under me and she spread her legs and wrapped them around me. This time we lapsed into a steady rhythmic motion, no less satisfying or satisfactory, until we reached the mutual orgasm that one seeks always and gets so seldom.

Early the next morning I was awakened by a knock on the door and the arrival of a maid bearing two breakfast trays. She evinced no sign of surprise at finding me sharing my bed, so I assumed that all the household staff had been well trained.

After breakfast I went into the bathroom for a shave and shower, leaving Tina to explain or not to explain why she was running around the house completely naked. My opinion was that the staff would look askance at her only if they didn't find a man in her bed. The rest of the day I submitted myself to Tina's tour of Montevideo and was impressed, surprised and aghast in turn, depending on the information I was fed. We had dinner back at the villa where the housekeeper turned out to be a very competent cook and made steady inroads on Tina's champagne supply.

Before we retired for the night Tina suggested a nightcap. I enthusiastically agreed: champagne is fine but I don't like a steady diet of it. I asked for a weak Scotch and water and we went out onto the terrace that overlooked the harbor with its reflection of the shipping lights mingled with the stars from the water. When our drinks were brought to us Tina said, "Would you mind very much if I left you alone tomorrow, Nick?"

"Of course not."

"We'll leave for the mine the day after tomorrow, and there are a few things I need to take care of before we start. It will give you a chance to go shopping."

"What do I need?"

"You're going to need a pair of sunglasses and a hat and I suggest you buy a gun. We'll be driving over some pretty rugged countryside."

"Driving?" I had expected to be flown there in a private aircraft.

"That's the only way to see the countryside. We'll take a Land Rover and take our time. Curtis can fly up in the helicopter."

"Why doesn't he come with us?"

"His time is too valuable. He had a great deal to do in Montevideo."

I said, "I'm surprised that your time isn't too valuable to take the time to drive there. Is it very far?"

"It's about a day's drive. Curtis will leave in the afternoon and fly up in the chopper. We'll spend the next day at the mine and return the following day."

She stood up and stifled an obviously staged yawn, "Then, let's get to bed."

I drained my drink and obediently trotted off with her to pay my board and lodging fees. Tina was a very innovative lover that night: perhaps she sensed my boredom and was making a special effort to keep me on the string. The next morning she left before I came out of the bathroom. I wandered down to the garage where I found I had a choice of a Cadillac or a Mercedes Benz 450SL; I took the Mercedes and thoroughly enjoyed the drive into town.

I had only been in Montevideo once before and it had been an assignment that kept me busy, so with that much time on my hands I felt free to wander round some of the quaint little streets. The first thing I did was to send an encoded telegram to Hawk telling him the current situation. I seemed to be wasting a lot of time but I had that intuitive feeling that the key to the whole gold-smuggling business was in Tina Rodriguez.

I found a clothing store and bought myself a bush jacket and a wide-brimmed hat, neither of which were to my personal taste but I felt that they boosted the image I was trying to create. The bush jacket came equipped with cartridge loops, but its main purpose was to cover my arms so that I could wear Hugo and hide Wilhelmina under its skirt. I walked out of the store wearing Hugo and the bush jacket and the hat which had a fake ocelot hat band. I was pleased with my appearance—I looked like a tourist who wanted to look like a great white hunter. My next stop was at a gunsmith's where I bought a box of 9mm snakeshot shells for Wilhelmina.

Many years ago the snakeshot cartridge was invented by a man who came face to face with a snake with nothing more lethal than a .38 pistol. A .38 pistol is a fine weapon but it's no match for a striking snake. A friend dispatched the snake with a shotgun blast and the idea of the snakeshot was born. The snakeshot cartridge is similar in every dimension to the standard shell, but instead of the lead slug it carries a clear plastic container which holds a full charge of lead shot. I was surprised that they were so readily available in 9mm in such an out-of-the-way location, but the 9mm caliber is growing ever more popular with sportsmen and target shooters.

With my shopping chores completed I stopped off at the post office to collect my mail. When I go undercover it is always a hit-and-miss affair trying to get in touch with Hawk. If I am out in the open I can stop off at any embassy and use the scrambler radio to call, but when I use a different identity I have to use the general delivery at the post office. I had been overly suspicious of Tina Rodriguez right from the start when Paul Winters had first mentioned her name and if I was being followed, which I strongly suspected, I would not dare to be seen entering an embassy. There is a very simple code that we use and I was expecting a telegram from Hawk indicating that he had received my telegrams and approved of my movements. When I came up empty-handed at the post office I was concerned. Hawk had stressed the fact that he was relying on me to keep him informed and if he had not received my telegrams then Tina Rodriguez or one of her staff had much further-reaching influence than I expected. Sufficiently far reaching to prevent my telegrams from arriving at their destination.

I decided that it was worth taking a chance on and I spent the next two hours shaking my unseen tail. I make my final move outside the embassy grounds and then walked in. Once inside it was only moments before I was seated at the radio calling Washington. Hawk wasn't in his office, but I spoke with his secretary.

"Debby, I'm a little worried. Has Mr. Hawk received my telegrams?"

"Yes, Mr. Carter. He was going to cable you as soon as he got on board."

"Did he leave town?" I suppose basically there was no reason why he should not take a vacation the same as the rest of us, particularly in view of the pressures of his job, but it seemed so strange to call and not have Hawk answer the phone himself.

"Mr. Hawk left town to supervise the security arrangements of the forthcoming peace talks."

"What peace talks are those?"

"I had forgotten that you had been out of town for a while. Our State Department is organizing peace talks between several South American nations, and Mr. Hawk has been charged with the responsiblity of the security arrangements."

"But he has received my telegrams and knows what I am doing?"

"Naturally I don't know what was in them, but he has received your telegrams."

"Thanks, Debby, and keep the coffee warm for me."

I switched off the set with a feeling of discontent. I certainly hadn't received the cable Hawk was intending to send me when he boarded his aircraft, but it may have got bogged down at Acapulco and was waiting to be forwarded to Montevideo. Stranger things than that have happened in South America. There was no reason why Hawk should keep me informed of his movements but I had a gut feel for it which was more than a feeling of dissatisfaction that Hawk wasn't there to back me up.

Leaving the embassy I walked several blocks to try to flush my tail, but I reached the Mercedes not having seen any sign of him. I slid behind the wheel and drove to the more dilapidated part of town, the section that promised so much for the intrepid explorer. Much of the displays were tourist bait and as usual I broke several overeager hearts by responding to pidgin English with fluent Spanish. I browsed around several stores with handcrafted silver ornaments, passed up a collection of wooden items that had been carved from the cross that Christ was crucified on and thumbed through a selection of patterned silks.

I noticed a pattern to the stores. I was particularly interested in the silver and goldsmiths since they were related to my assignment and I noticed that the further I got from the main drag where all the commercial establishments were, the more shoddy was the workmanship of the goods for sale. At the same time perhaps, one out of every four stores away from the main street offered up a certain originality as though to make up for the poor workmanship. If they didn't have it in their hands, it seemed, they made up for it with their creative skills.

I turned down a wide street and followed the silversmiths, watching them at work casting, engraving, polishing and working the heated malleable metal. I turned down several offers to make me an engraved identity bracelet and watched an old man forging the links in a chain destined to glamorize the neck of some social misfit. All the silk shops had disappeared and now there were very few silversmiths about. I came to an alley and, fascinated by the progression of goldsmithing, I turned into it.

The alley was paved with slabs of stone that probably dated back to 1836 when the city was revitalized and was so narrow I could have stood in the middle and touched both walls with my fingertips. Now, I was in the heart of the goldsmithing business. Stretched out on either side of me were long lengths of goldsmithing workbenches. I had passed the point where they had window displays, as a matter of fact I had passed the point where they had windows. Each man was sitting out in the open at a workbench with a cloth spread out to catch the trimmings. They sat in front of single-story buildings which probably held their families and all their worldly possessions and worked their precious metals. Each one, I suspected, with a razor-sharp machete under the bench within easy reach of his hand to discourage thieves. There was a code among them and if any stranger had paused to pick up a piece of gold trimming he would have found himself looking down at his severed hand sliced off by the machete.

With my fascination for the workings taking place in front of me I lost track of my surroundings, until I realized that I had passed the last of the goldsmiths and was in an area of rundown shacks. They were probably the homes of the shop clerks and craftsmen who were employed by the stores I had just passed. There didn't seem to be much point in continuing so I turned to retrace my steps. As I turned I heard a sound above me.

I looked up and saw a net being flung over me. It was spread wide and its weight carried me down to my knees and entangled my arms and legs. I flexed the muscles of my right arm which sent Hugo shooting down into my waiting palm. I slashed out at the net and as I did so two men landed beside me and threw an evil-smelling blanket over my head.

I redoubled my efforts to cut myself loose. I was off balance which prevented me from getting a good slashing blow. I thrust up at the net and the blanket beyond it and was rewarded with a stifled scream as Hugo's needle-sharp point found its mark in somebody's hide. I kicked out at where I thought the other assailant should be but my legs were inextricably entangled in the net. I reached down and swept Hugo from side to side just about my ankles until my legs were free. I put the full psychophysical force into a karate kick aimed at where my adversary should be. I heard a grunt and suddenly the hands holding me were released.

I struggled to my feet, kicking away at what was left of the net and blanket. By the time I was free of my encumbrances there was no sign of my attackers. I stopped a man passing by and asked him if he had seen anything. "Quien sabe?" he answered. "Who the hell cares?"

FOUR

I picked up my newly acquired hat and slapped it on my thigh to remove some of the dust, perched it on my head and started to walk back to where I had left the Mercedes. I drove back to the villa without further incident and joined Tina and Curtis on the terrace for cocktails.

I was invited to recount my day's activities. With the exception of the visit to the embassy for which I substituted a visit to the renowned plazas, the Zabala, the Independencia and the Constitucion I faithfully reported my day's movements. The narrative ended in the true storytelling style with the unprovoked attack on me. Both Tina and McBride were quick to blame my appearance as the cause.

McBride said, "Montevideo is not the place it used to be. It's becoming as bad as New York."

While Tina commented, "There people are all peasants and to them any American is easy pickings."

It was time to add to my image. "If they'd point a

gun at me or a good sharp knife they could have had my wallet. I'm not about to try to be a hero. What do they say? Better a live coward than a dead hero. Well you can put me at the top of your list of live cowards."

"It was all your fault," McBride told me, "you should never have gone into that part of town. Anybody would have told you that section is dangerous."

I said, "All I did was to wander through the shops and a silversmith caught my eye, and before I knew it I was in the goldsmiths' section. I'm kind of surprised that there should be that kind of violence in a part of town that should be noted for its security arrangements."

I had my own ideas of who was responsible for the attacks. My favorite was the guy who had been tailing me all day, the one I had tried unsuccessfully to flush out. The other thing that bothered me was the net. If I had been intended to play the victim of a mugging, why the net? Of course it could have been some enemy of AXE or myself. My job is not conducive to making lifelong friends among the people I come in contact with in the course of a normal day's work. But if it was an old enemy of mine or AXE, why try to capture me alive. They hadn't used such discriminatory methods when they had disposed of Dennis Gordon. The attack had come from the rooftops and it would have been easier to shoot me from there than to drop a net over me to try to take me alive. After all, one well-placed shot and all he needed to do was to jump down and grab my watch and wallet, and that wouldn't take more than one man. That gave me enough to think about while Tina and McBride turned the conversation to the output of the mine.

During dinner I was able to keep up my end of the conversation with accounts of what I had seen in Montevideo and what I remembered having read about it. That's the nice thing about having a photographic memory, I can always slip little snippets of information into the dialogue and give the impression that I have just seen it, whereas I might have read about it many years ago. The conversation at the dinner table was hardly inspirational and as soon as I decently could I asked for a nightcap. Curtis McBride wholeheartedly agreed with me and Tina fell in with the majority.

It was about time for Tina to suggest our going to bed when she caught me by surprise. She put her glass down and said, "Tell me about the silversmiths, Nick."

"What silversmiths?"

"The ones you watched today."

"I can't tell you much about them. There were quite a few of them. I was first attracted to a guy who was making rings, then further on there were a couple making belt buckles, and by that time I was in the middle of the goldsmithing section."

"What were they doing."

"Mostly shaping the heated metal. They all had a little furnace that they used to keep the metal hot." I went into a lengthy description of the old man who had been shaping the links of a gold chain, giving the impression that I had watched several artisans performing the same chore.

Unless Tina was as suspicious of me as I was of her it should not have been necessary to test me out, unless she had received word that I had visited the embassy. She had not received any phone calls or messages since

I had joined her and McBride, but there had been ample time for my shadow to have called while I was on my way back in the Mercedes. On reflection, if my suspicions were correct my attackers in the alley may have called her.

"So you think the silversmithing was fascinating, do you?" she asked.

"Absolutely, but not so fascinating as the goldsmithing. Perhaps because there is so much more inherent value in the base metal."

"I'm glad you like it because you're going to see a lot of it tomorrow."

"Tomorrow? I thought we were going to the mine tomorrow."

"We are," said McBride, "but why do you think we have a mine?"

"To get lead to sell on the open market."

"Wrong. We do mine lead but it's a losing proposition. We supply lead for batteries, paint and for roofing materials; but lead is indestructible and all the lead used in batteries is reclaimed as well as roofing materials is reclaimed. I expect very shortly somebody will come up with a method of reclaiming the lead oxides used in paint. The money we make on lead would not pay the wages of our mining staff."

"Then why?"

"The lead we use for the souvenir castings up in Mexico City just barely pays its way. The real money we make is from the by-products."

"Like what?"

"The silver we mine along with the lead pays for the whole mining operation, and the gold we get is the icing on the cake."

"That's very interesting," I said. "I can't wait to get up to the mine to see it for myself."

That was a gross exaggeration; I wanted to see if Tina and her company were pulling enough gold out of the ground to shatter the gold market in the States as well as supplying her with enough money to live like a millionairess.

It was about time I took the initiative in our lovemaking to allay her suspicions. I put my empty glass down and stood up. "I guess we can talk about that tomorrow at more length when we get to the mine. Right now I'm ready for bed."

I led the way to the bedroom where I stripped off before turning my attention to Tina. Before I was undressed she had wriggled out of her evening dress and was standing there clad only in her panties. I pushed her down onto the bed and slid her panties off. She put her arms round my neck and pulled my face down to her chest. Her nipples were dark red and distended with desire. I buried my face between her breasts but she pulled my head to one side and guided a hard rubberlike nipple between my lips. I slid my hand down to her thighs. She rolled over and spread her legs offering her secret place to my touch; it felt wet and inviting. I rolled over onto her and she clamped her legs around me as I penetrated her.

We fell into an easy rhythm and I could feel the moist warmth of her gripping me while I pumped into her. I stepped up the pace while she braced herself even more tightly and suddenly we were lost in the frenzy of the movement until I exploded inside her and we groaned in mutual ecstasy.

The next morning I shaved, showered and dressed

before the maid brought the breakfast tray. For a change I went downstairs to the dining room and joined Curtis McBride for the morning meal before Tina put in her appearance for champagne and orange juice. Although I was anxious to bring up the subject of gold again to find out what I could, McBride seemed reluctant to respond to any conversational gambit, remaining engrossed in the file he held.

After breakfast I went outside to find a Japanese version of the Land Rover at the foot of the steps. It had already been packed with a strange suitcase and my flight bag. I was wearing Hugo under the sleeve of my bush jacket and Wilhelmina was on my belt out of sight. I checked the spare cans of gas and water. In addition to the spare wheel bolted to the tailgate we carried another on the roof. Under the hood everything seemed to be in order and I went back inside for a last cup of coffee with Tina before leaving. She was also outfitted in a bush jacket and a wide-brimmed hat.

Tina finished her coffee and then went upstairs, promising to meet me at the vehicle. I thought she was going to make a last minute trip to the bathroom, but when she came out she was carrying an Interarms Mark X Marquis rifle in 7x57mm caliber. I had been told that we would be driving over rugged terrain but I hadn't expected it to be that rugged.

As she put the rifle into the clamps that were provided on the dashboard she answered my startled look. "Parts of Uruguay are still very primitive and there is always the possibility of running into a jaguar."

We left with me doing the driving and Tina calling the turns until we got out of town and settled down to the main road that would take us from the Rio de la Plata and into the surrounding countryside. I had been told that it was rugged territory and that was no overstatement. The road itself was little more than a rough track which had been made by the passage of a great many vehicles, most of them drawn by mules, horses or oxen. Fortunately the Land Rover's springing was up to the beating it was getting and we were able to ride out the rough road without getting our spines shattered.

I was puzzled as to why Tina wanted to show me the countryside. There was nothing to see along the way except for an occasional crude hut and groups of children who took time out from their playing to wave enthusiastically. Once or twice a bus passed forcing us off to the side of the road to avoid the clouds of dust. On these occasions there was a great deal of humanity to be seen with people packed into every available space and clinging to the old-fashioned running boards. On the second passing of a bus, the luggage rack surmounted on the roof, besides a motley collection of suitcases and cloth-wrapped bundles, carried two crates of chickens. They were white chickens as I was reminded every time I plucked a feather out of my nose for the next several days.

For a millionairess who was accustomed to living on champagne and having a team of servants at her beck and call, Tina was absorbing the rough ride very well. I expected her to be bitching every time anything interfered with her comfort, but when the bus passed, showering us with chicken feathers, she actually laughed as though it was great sport. Maybe I could learn something from her.

We stopped for lunch at a natural widening of the road. One of those places where buses pass each other and where not so many years ago, mule teams did the same. We were in mining country now and on either side of us were heaps of earth that had been drained of any sign of precious metal and left to waste away. In several places small trees could be seen to have taken root in these piles of earth. We found a spot as far from the beaten track as possible and settled down in the shade of a gigantic magnolia tree.

Beyond the piles of earth where the mine workings had not ravaged the land, the countryside was covered with grass, liberally interspersed with wild flowers and I saw innumerable flocks of sheep. We lunched on cold chicken and the inevitable cold champagne. After lunch we climbed back on board ready for the last leg of the trip which I was told would take us through the pasture lands. It was January and the air was temperate, mildly pleasant as opposed to the searing heat that would plague Australia at the time of the year or the humidity I have found in other parts of the southern hemisphere. There was no breeze and sound carried a long way.

Before I shattered the silence with the noise of the Land Rover's engine I heard a sound. I cocked my head to hear better. Did you hear a car start up?"

"A car?" Tina repeated, looking puzzled. "Not out here. The only vehicles we might see are buses."

I strained my ears but if I had heard correctly the noise of the starter had died down to a mere rumble of the engine, inaudible from that distance.

I started up the engine and drove us back onto the

road again. The only vehicle in sight was a load of freshly shorn sheepskins powered by a splay-footed mule guided by a ten-year-old boy, although there was some doubt in my mind as to who was guiding whom. The boy waved to us as we passed but the mule kept all four feet firmly planted on the ground. I watched them out of sight in my mirror.

The mine workings had given way now to the pastoral scene, which made for more pleasant surroundings. Just before the mule disappeared from view I saw the lad guide him over to the side of the road and step clear as a cloud of dust came on the scene. Suddenly it started to rain—a short, sharp shower. I turned on my windshield wipers and my headlights to make sure that no one would mistake the Land Rover for a wandering mule. Whatever it was behind us it had not yet reached the rain and was still hidden by the dust cloud, progressively coming closer.

I pointed it out to Tina who looked back but made no comment. The brief shower finished and I saw the mirror that our pursuers had reached the dampened ground. Instead of a cloud of dust I could see an ancient car; it looked like a 1950 Ford, one of the first to extend the trunk from the aerodynamically rear end. I was puzzling as to why anybody would want to drive a car of that vintage at such a bone-shattering speed, but I didn't stay puzzled for long. Now that he had left the cloud of dust behind him I could see that it was a convertible and that the top was down and that the passenger was standing up leveling a rifle at us.

Even from that distance, the shot came to us as a clean, clear sound like a whip cracking but the bullet went hopelessly astray. It was impossible to line up the sights on an object so much in constant motion as the Land Rover was, and the instability of his own car compounded the error but that didn't stop him from trying. For the next few seconds a fusillade of shots rang out, none of them coming close enough to hit the vehicle or make a disturbance in the road.

I pointed to the rifle that was clamped to the dashboard and said to Tina, "Let's see how good you are with that thing. Tell me when you're ready, and I'll slow down a bit."

Our assailant had reloaded by this time and the shots started all over again. He wasn't hitting anything so maybe he was trying to scare us to death. Tina leveled the rifle over the back of the seat and told me to slow down a bit. I slapped the brakes on and checked our speed over the ruts, expecting to hear the whipcrack of the Marquis, but got nothing.

I picked up our speed and reached out and took the rifle from her grasp. Then, clamping the steering wheel between my knees I ejected the magazine. It was completely empty.

"What were you planning to do if we met a jaguar?" I asked. "Shove it up his ass and say boo?"

"I told them to load it for me."

"You never tell anyone to load a gun for you. A gun is meant to save your life, so you need to take the responsibility of loading it yourself. Where's the rest of the ammunition?"

"I guess I don't have any. I thought one magazine full would be plenty."

"It probably would have been if you'd loaded it yourself."

"Somebody's going to get fired for that."

"Which will leave him a lot better off than us when those sons of bitches catch up with us."

With my slowing down to steady us for Tina's shot the car behind was no more than a hundred yards away. Either he had got used to the rifle or he was too close to miss because the next shot shattered my outside mirror.

"They're pretty good with a gun," I said. "Let's see what kind of courage they have without it. Brace yourself."

Tina was wearing a seat belt and with her feet firmly braced against the floor I pulled up on the hand brake which locked the back wheels and spun the Land Rover through a hundred-and-eighty-degree turn. Facing my pursuers I released the hand brake and clamped down on the gas pedal. To the surprise of Tina and our pursuers we were heading straight at them on a collision course.

The driver wavered, not sure of what was going to happen. I corrected my course and when the Rover was aimed directly at him I clamped down on the gas pedal. On that rough track I couldn't get the speed I would have liked but it served its purpose. I must confess to being able to credit my education with my responses. The two guys in the other car had obviously never played "chicken."

As soon as the driver saw my intention he weaved from side to side then corrected his course while his passenger reloaded his rifle. I turned the car directly toward him and he corrected again. I flipped it down a gear and aimed it straight at him with the engine racing. It was too much for the other driver. We were on the left side of the track. He tried to get on the other side where he could pass me, but I cut him off like a good quarter horse with a rambunctious steer. He came back to my side of the road and within seconds he swung the wheel off to the right, climbed the bank and rammed into a giant magnolia tree.

I drifted around back to my original course and passed them with a derisive gesture. Apparently the passenger had more guts than the driver because in less than a hundred yards he started shooting again. He fired several shots that went wide but finally found his mark. Just as I thought I was getting out of range I felt the unmistakable thump as one of our tires went flat. I let the Land Rover go thumping along for another hundred yards so that I would not be too easy a target to hit and pulled off to the side behind a gigantic oak tree.

My last glimpse of our followers showed them to be trying to extricate themselves from the magnolia tree. The natural reaction of a driver who sees that he is about to run into something is to slow down to lessen the impact. Of course that does not apply to the game of chicken where you goad your opponent into going as fast as possible. I had no idea how fast he had been going when he hit; if I was lucky he would be put out of action permanently, and if my luck didn't hold he would be back to continue the chase.

"They've got it out from under the tree, Nick," she said moments later. "They've got the engine running again."

I threw the flat tire into the back and went to work on the lugs holding the spare in place. "Something's wrong. They've opened the hood and are looking inside."

We were standing on a slope and as I dropped the spare to the ground, it took off down the hill with me in hot pursuit, taking me out of the shelter of the oak tree. That was too much of a temptation and the rifle cracked again and the bullet ploughed up a furrow at my feet. I grabbed the rebellious wheel and scampered back behind the tree. I saw two bullets plunge into the earth where I had been standing before I got back to safety.

It was only seconds before I had the spare on and the Land Rover under way again, leaving the rifleman and his driver to do their best with their car.

FIVE

We continued on without wasting any time, and I thoroughly expected our trackers to give up. But that was not the case. I glanced in my mirror and the Ford was following us again a couple of hundred yards away. "I guess I'm going to have to stop playing games with them," I told Tina.

I waited until we reached a stretch of road that was free from children playing and mules going about their business. I pulled over to the side, climbed out and fished Wilhelmina from her holster under the skirt of my bush jacket. Steading myself against the Land Rover, I squeezed off two shots in rapid succession when the Ford got to within about fifty yards. "You missed," Tina said from her vantage point behind our vehicle as I climbed back in again.

"I didn't miss. I wasn't aiming at the driver. I was trying to hit the radiator." I pulled away and picked up our speed again. "You won't see anything for a while, but when sufficient water leaks out the car will overheat. And there's no way they can repair a leaking radiator this far from civilization.''

Within five minutes Tina reported that they had pulled off to the side of the road and stopped in a cloud of steam. With them out of the way I settled down to a restful drive with nothing on my mind except the off chance of meeting a jaguar with nothing more potent than an unloaded rifle and my good friend Wilhelmina.

We reached the turnoff which was brought to my attention not only by signs proclaiming the *Rodriguez Lead Mine* spelled out in English and Spanish but by Tina's excited squeals. The side road was extremely narrow and overgrown because, as Tina pointed out, the only traffic was the supply truck that visited once a week and occasional transport for workers leaving on their annual vacation to visit with their families, or new workers being brought to the site. We reached the cluster of huts just before sundown and I was introduced to Pedro Sanchez, the on-site manager.

We had barely off-loaded the case of champagne to be stored in the refrigerator when Curtis McBride arrived in the company helicopter. We sat down to a roughly prepared but wholesome meal that reflected the surroundings with Sanchez, McBride and Fellowes, the American who was the helicopter pilot. The talk over dinner was naturally about the production of the mine and I got the impression from what Sanchez said that the silver content had rapidly dwindled far below what had been expected and there was some talk between Sanchez and McBride about starting another shaft to see if they could pick up a new vein of silver. It was not until after dinner when Tina asked for the third bottle of champagne to be broached that she mentioned the attack on us. They listened politely but nobody seemed shocked.

I said, "I guess I'm the only one surprised."

"This is a rougher country than you expected," McBride said.

"What bothers me is that this is the second attempt to capture me alive in two days."

Sanchez remarked, "There are always bandidos in this area, and anybody could be carrying a haul of silver around here."

"They could take it off my dead body without capturing me."

"What makes you say that, Nick?"

"The attempt yesterday when they tried to capture me with a net, and today, when they shot at me all the bullets hit the ground at my feet, almost as though they were afraid of hitting me."

Tina said, "Maybe they recognized me."

"So what?"

"I'm well known in Uruguay as a millionairess, well worth kidnapping, and to these ignorant bandidos all Americans are rich. It was probably a kidnap attempt."

The others agreed with her, but I didn't voice my opinion. The biggest argument I could think of was Dennis Gordon who had had his throat slashed. There had been no attempt to kidnap Dennis, so why would they try to take me alive?

Before we broke up I said to Sanchez, "We came here with an empty rifle. Could I get some ammunition before we leave?"

"Sure. What caliber?"

"7x57mm for the Interarms Marquis in the Land Rover."

"That we don't have. We've got .30-06, .308 Winchester and .300 Magnum, but we don't have any of the metric sizes."

"Maybe I could borrow a rifle for the ride back."

I didn't want to declare my suspicions, but it seemed highly unlikely that Tina would bring an empty rifle with us when we were going to be shot at and then find that the caliber was one that couldn't be matched at the mine. If I had been suspicious of her before I was doubly so now, the only thing was that I couldn't think of any motive.

If my surmise that she was behind this gold smuggling was correct, then they certainly didn't need to take me alive. I could have been ambushed and dispatched the way Dennis Gordon had been.

After dinner Tina showed me a large cabin set apart from the others. From the look of it and with the photographs of the tired looking woman and three teen-agers I guessed it to be Sanchez's cabin, sacrificed for the boss while he spent the night in the dormitory with the mine workers. The sum total of the ablution facilities was a pitcher of water and an enamel bowl. For anything more basic there was a hike of a hundred yards to the screened off of the most primitive of holes in the ground. I noted that in deference to Tina's sex, Sanchez had posted a guard to prevent her from being interrupted.

When she returned to our cabin and started to undress I made the same trip myself. It had been dark for several hours by this time but the air was still warm and dry. It was a clear night and I could see all the stars of the southern hemisphere. A slight breeze rustled through the tree tops and the entire atmosphere was one of tranquility. I performed whatever had to be done and started back again to the cabin, marvelling at the serenity which was such a far cry from the environment around my apartment in Washington.

I had gone no further than thirty or forty feet when the rustling in the trees above me increased. My first thought was of a jaguar or wildcat, but I decided it was highly unlikely that either would attack without extreme provocation. Probably some kind of bird I told myself.

As I passed the tree where all the noise was coming from, the rustling intensified and I heard the twin thuds of a heavy two-legged animal hit the ground. I whirled to meet my attacker and as I did, there was the sound of a second man jumping to the ground on the other side of me. The moon had not yet risen, but by the light of the stars I could see a man crouched before me holding what appeared to be a club. On my left his partner similarly armed was approaching me with his weapon held high.

I didn't wait for him to swing at me but shifted my weight to my right foot and slammed my left foot into his stomach. The other man darted in to take advantage of my being off balance. He swung at my head but I ducked back, grabbed his club and pulled him toward me. As he blundered past I tripped him and sent him sprawling into his partner. I adopted the *kempo* stance, the defensive pose and waited for them to disentangle themselves. With one of them winded I didn't expect much of an attack, but both of them had one more try.

The first man shifted his club from his right hand to the left, presumably to confuse me, and then swung it at my kidney. I shot my feet out from under me and kicked him solidly in the nuts. He collapsed in a heap leaving the other still trying to get enough air to continue the attack by himself. He came forward a little more slowly trying to connect with my head now that I was on the ground. If he expected me to lie there like a golf ball while he swung at me he had miscalculated. I rolled over letting the club swish past my head and jabbed up with three rigid fingers at the nerve point at the back of his elbow. He dropped the club and brought his other arm up to protect himself. His right arm hung loosely by his side. I slashed leisurely at his face with the edge of my right hand, and when he raised his left arm to ward off the blow I struck hard and uncompromisingly with my balled left fist at the side of his neck.

He collapsed in a heap over the body of his comrade who was still holding his balls. I reached down and lifted him high enough by his shirt front to launch a karate kick at the other man. Then I continued my unhurried stroll back to the cabin for a night of love-making on one of the lumpiest mattresses I have ever slept on. Fortunately for my comfort I spent almost the entire night on top.

I made no mention of the attack either to Tina that night or to the others at breakfast the next morning. I was thoroughly convinced by now that either Tina or Curtis McBride had masterminded all these attempts, and if I mentioned them I would be met with excuses about bandidos trying to rob me. I can see muggers looking for victims in the public toilets in New York, but not in the wilds of Uruguay. What I needed to do was to find out their motive in capturing me unharmed. If I told them about it and they were guilty they would deny it, and if they were innocent they could consider me paranoid. I thought it better to let things run their course.

I had devoured a man-sized portion of hotcakes and about half a pint of coffee when Sanchez produced a file of reports. He, McBride and Tina gathered round the breakfast table while I was given over to the charge of Catarina Montez, one of the foremen, for a tour of the mine.

Cat Montez was a colorful character. He was the product of a wandering sailor and a part-time whore and had been brought up in a succession of foster homes in his home town of Lima, Peru. He had run away from at the age of fourteen and had followed in his father's footsteps as a sailor. He very soon grew tired of the rigorous winters spent rounding the Horn and went looking for a job that would provide him with a steady income and a chance to settle down. He signed a contract with one of the Peruvian lead mines and started to learn the business from the ground up. By the very nature of their work lead miners live a hermitlike existence, and in one of his infrequent trips to town he got raving drunk and got into a fight over some broad.

Like most sailors Cat always carried a knife, and the next morning he found himself wanted by the police for murder. He hadn't very much faith in the Peruvian system of justice and stowed away on a freighter bound for Montevideo. As soon as he was discovered he was put to work and gave a pretty good account of himself. At Montevideo he jumped ship figuring that the full width of the continent couldn't be too much spacc between himself and the police. He was reluctant to go back to sea in case one of his vessels made an unscheduled trip to Lima and delivered him into the hands of the police.

The way he saw it he had no option but to take up his alternative vocation of lead mining. The Rodriguez Lead Mine had been only too anxious to hire a lead miner with previous experience and he rapidly rose to the position of foreman. He seemed to be well liked by the men, and he obviously had the confidence of Sanchez who had delivered me into his hands.

Cat showed me where the basic ore, called galena, was crushed and blended to make various oxides, and how they extracted the copper, zinc and silver. There were several silversmiths at work and he explained that silver working was a very lucrative subsidiary of the mine which paid the entire cost of running the mine.

"How about the gold?" I aked.

"Not here in Uruguay," he told me. "It is very common to find gold with galena, but not in Uruguay. The lead in Peru is very rich in gold, and so is that of the United States I am told, but here in Uruguay we never see gold."

I didn't feel that I should pursue the subject. It certainly didn't answer the question in my mind and I felt that rather than getting closer to a solution I was getting away from it. I now had two questions on my mind. Why was somebody trying to capture me alive, and why had Tina and McBride lied to me about the gold they mined in Uruguay. There was one more question I could ask Montez without letting my suspicions show.

I said, "Does *Señora* Rodriguez have other lead mines besides this one?"

"Oh, *si, señor*. This is only one of many."

"Here in Uruguay?"

"I believe this is the only one in Uruguay. She has two or three in Peru and I believe one or two in Ecuador and Bolivia."

Perhaps they were mining more gold on the West Coast, but the output from Uruguay would hardly be enough to make her a millionairess. Although I had only my own assumption that she was a millionairess from the gold she was mining. She had certainly mentioned her industries, and industry can be very lucrative.

I stayed down the mine and had lunch with the workers before finishing the tour. I had no more questions to ask and I concentrated on absorbing as much information as possible. I found Cat Montez a very likable person and under other circumstances I might have enjoyed his company on a night on the town. He returned me to the main camp in time for cocktails before dinner.

Sanchez played the host and mixed Scotch and water for myself and McBride and opened a bottle of champagne for Tina, but she changed her mind at the last moment and took Scotch. Sanchez drank a colorless liquid, that was probably tequila.

The cook came up with an enormous bowl of venison stew which was as good as any I have tasted anywhere.

Apparently their business meeting had been successful; everybody was in a good mood and Sanchez was kept busy replenishing the glasses.

I was asked my impression of the mine and was able to impart much of the knowledge I had gleaned from Montez. It was a great temptation to bring up the question of the gold, particularly since it had been McBride who had brought up the subject in the first place. If Tina was not pulling gold out of the ground she could not have been smuggling it into the States unless she had another source. But if one didn't mine gold, where the hell did one get it from in such quantities?

The conversation over the dinner table was on a par with that of the previous evening, and this was followed by an evening of social chitchat with Sanchez acting as bartender. I don't know if Tina's champagne supply had run out but she had switched entirely to Scotch. In any event it did nothing to deplete her passion later that night.

We all took the tour of the mine the next day with Sanchez leading and Cat Montez bringing up the rear. I half expected another attempt to be made on me under cover of the darkness that is inherent in a mine. For that reason I kept well back. I had an intuitive feeling of trust for Cat Montez and if anything should happen to me I would feel more confident if he was near. The evening was a repetition of the previous one. The cook whose ingenuity had not been tried for so long made a roast rack of lamb garnished with potatoes au gratin that would have done any New York chef proud.

After another passionate night we left after an ample breakfast of ham and eggs. The Interarms Marquis had vanished and in its place stood a Weatherly .300 Magnum, a match for any prowling jaguar or stalking kidnapper.

Much to my surprise the drive back to Tina's villa was without incident. I had confidently expected at least one more try before we got back to civilization, but it was more in the nature of a Sunday School picnic than a day in the life of an AXE operative.

SIX

As peaceful as was the drive back to the villa there was an unpleasant surprise waiting for me. There was a reception committee consisting of Al, Willie Chan and the peroxide blonde. Apparently they formed the usual escort service and it was only on rare occasions that they were left behind.

This gave me even more food for thought. Why had Tina elected to take only me with her to Montevideo? Was it to set me up for the kidnapping attempt? It should have been just as easy to have left me in Acapulco, but I doubted that Al or Willie Chan could have pulled it off. It still didn't answer my question on the motive. Of course, had I questioned why I had been selected to make the trip I would have been given the tongue-in-cheek protestations of undying love, and I can get along very well without undying love.

Everybody slipped into what was the normal routine for them. Curtis McBride arrived later just before dinner, but in the meantime the other three fell into a hard-drinking pattern. I tried to get into the conversation but it was difficult. Gonsalez, the peroxide blonde, had nothing on her mind except women's fashions, a subject that didn't interest me. When Tina wasn't talking about fashions she and Curtis McBride had their heads together discussing business.

Under normal circumstances I would have been bored stiff, and the only reason I hung in there was the thought of Dennis Gordon and Hawk's concern about the gold smuggling. I managed to weather the boredom of the dinner and when Tina started to talk fashion again I suggested a game of chess to McBride. He agreed with alacrity but turned out to be a very poor player.

I beat him soundly while Al and Willie Chan looked on. It take a certain amount of brain to understand the game and from the expression on their faces they had been briefed not to make waves. They feigned interest which is not easy to do when you haven't the slightest idea of what is going on. I was almost relieved when Tina proclaimed that she was tired and indicated an early night.

The next morning we left the others sleeping and took a pitcher of champagne and orange juice down to the pool. After a few laps we climbed out and Tina rang the bell to have breakfast served poolside. Somewhere between the grapefruit and the cold cereal she turned to me and said, "Tomorrow we'll be going on to Mexico City."

"To see your industries?"

"Actually to see just one of them."

"Which one is that?"

"The foundry where we cast the lead into ornamental toreadors, matadors and bulls to sell to the tourists at Tijuana, El Paso, Mexicali, Nogales and such places."

"So, although all your industries are south of the border, you still make your money from the Americans."

"Like every businessman we cater to the potential customer. In this case most of the customers are American."

"I thought you had an entire string of industries in Mexico."

"I do, but this one is a very special one."

"How so?"

"When I first started to get interested in Alvin's businesses we had a small foundry where we used to cast battery plates. I saw the potential of it and Alvin gave me a free hand. The souvenir figurines were my idea. Not only was it my idea but I did much of the layout of the factory with the help of a couple of engineers."

"It sounds pretty successful."

"I'm very proud of it."

"So you should be. I've never done anything constructive in my life."

"It's probably because you haven't had the opportunity."

"I'm just not an idea man."

"I wouldn't say that, Nick." I wondered then if she had heard the report from the two guys who had tried unsuccessfully to waylay me at the mine. But on second thought I doubted it. Those sort of reports are always strongly biased to make the one who is doing the reporting appear in the best light. She had seen first hand how I dealt with the intending kidnappers on the way out to the mine, and if it had been the same two men they would have been content to let the matter rest.

Tina had decided to take me on another tour of the city for the rest of that day. I would be forced to give the others the slip in order to make a call to Hawk. It had already been far too long since I had talked with him.

Tina had ordered a limousine to transport the five of us; Curtis McBride was apparently excused to devote all his time to the running of the business interests. For a while there, I regretted my decision to play the role of the playboy. The part of a businessman would have given me considerably more freedom. Tina sent one of the servants to wake the others up and we went back into the pool to while away the not inconsiderable time that it took them to prepare themselves for an appearance in public.

When they finally showed themselves at the breakfast table, Tina and I took off for a shower and to dress. We all tumbled into the limousine and I was disappointed to find that we were heading in the opposite direction to the embassy. I had hoped to be able to use an excuse like going shopping and getting lost. I tried it to see if it would work but she ordered Willie Chan to accompany me because he knew where all the right shops were. I gave my expense account a beating trying to keep the playboy image.

Willie Chan didn't make a nuisance of himself, he just stayed by my side and I took it out on him by making him carry all my packages. Once was enough, the point had been made. I knew that I would not be able to duck away from the others when we got closer to the embassy. But I had to get word to Hawk somehow.

We stopped for what in anybody else's language would have been a coffee break but in our case was a round of highballs. The entire trip was given over to Tina's homemade lecture tour with Gonsalez contributing some minor historical information. They had their act down pretty pat. I would have been convinced that they were simply trying to show the wandering tourist the sights had it not been for the fact Willie Chan was detailed to accompany me. I guess Tina knew better than to send Al.

Sometime in the early afternoon we passed a large shopping center and I expressed a very natural tourist desire to go look around. I was sent off with Willie Chan breathing down my neck. I browsed around and bought several more trinkets and then expressed an urgent need to find a rest room. Willie Chan knew exactly where it was and escorted me up to the third floor of a large department store. I had hoped to leave him outside but he came in with me. I loaded him up with packages and took the middle of three cubicles.

I sat down, took my notebook from my pocket and hastily encoded a note to Hawk telling him that I was about to continue my trip to Mexico City. Across the top I wrote the Spanish equivalent of telegram and waited for somebody to occupy one of the neighboring cubicles.

Eventually I heard the door on my right open and a pair of shoes make their appearance under the space at the bottom of the divider. The shoes were well polished and equally well worn and the pants were of some cheap synthetic fiber such as a shop clerk might wear, which was ideal for my purpose. A shop clerk would not be above taking a bribe of the size I intended to offer and would be able to read and understand what I expected of him.

I folded five one-thousand peso notes fanwise—that was almost the equivalent of five hundred American dollars—and pushed them up under the divider. When I felt his fingers brush them I withdrew them and offered my note. It was taken from my fingers, there was a short pause while he read it and then the fingers came down under the divider again. I gave him the money, flushed the toilet and came out to wash my hands where Willie Chan could see me, hoping that I had made a good choice and that the guy would not take my money and run.

We returned to the limousine without further comment and I was expected to display my purchases. Very shortly after that we wound up the tour and returned to the villa, me for a swim and the others to continue with their drinking. The housekeeper/cook had a very unstable position never knowing when her mistress would be arriving or departing, but she seemed to have the matter well in hand for dinner that night with roast duck which I was assured had only been shot that morning. Again I had the temptation to ask if the guy who loaded the shotgun was the same one who was supposed to load the rifle for our trip to the mine. If there was game shooting within reach of the villa I did not know why I hadn't been informed of it. This compounded my suspicions even further; why should they take such intricate steps to prevent me from getting a loaded gun in my hands. That thought took root and I worried all through dinner when I made my excuses and went to the bathroom to strip Wilhelmina and check her out. A buddy of mine had once got involved with some broad and when he found himself in a tight spot, the firing pin of his gun had been filed off. Wilhelmina was in excellent shape, so maybe nobody had thought of it yet.

Because of the traveling we were scheduled for the following day Tina called for an early night, stressing the fact that the others would need to be up early. That statement was greeted by sour looks but no objections were raised. After all, what the hell could they object to when they were just along for a free ride.

We were up early the next morning and for a change there were six of us at the breakfast table. I had half expected Curtis McBride to be left behind to attend to his vice-presidential duties, but he formed one of the group that was driven to the airport to catch a regularly scheduled flight into Mexico City. At the airport we were met by the Rolls Royce and the chauffeur we had left in Acapulco, so it was apparently a part of the regular entourage and had been flown over while we were in Montevideo. All I could guess from that was that either Tina was planning on staying in Mexico City for a while or she intended to return to Acapulco.

SEVEN

Even if she was not taking a fortune out of the ground with the gold, there was no denying that Tina had millions at her disposal. The villa at Mexico City was every bit as plush as the one at Montevideo. There was an Olympic-sized swimming pool and the neatly manicured lawns and shrubs attested to the fact that there was a full-time staff employed.

The following morning we lapsed into the same old routine. Champagne and orange juice and breakfast beside the pool before the sun got too hot. This time I wasn't given the tour of the city, which was just as well; I know Mexico City as well as any non-native and it would have been easy to let something slip revealing my knowledge when I wasn't supposed to know anything of Mexico. I was taken straight to the foundry which was Tina's pride and joy. It covered at least a half a block and was squeezed in between a rubber processing plant, which was making retreads and recaps, and an auto upholsterer advertising a special on completely upholstering any American car in "genuine simulated ocelot fur."

The Rolls pulled in beside a stake truck that was being loaded with crates, and McBride, Tina and I climbed out. The Rolls backed out and took off. I had noticed a telephone beside the driver, so he was never more than a phone call away. I followed the other two into the main entrance and into the big office. I pride myself on being able to read the expressions on people's faces and I could see that our visit was unexpected, but everybody was pleased to see Tina. She introduced me around and I could not help but notice that she called everyone by their first name. With several of the women she stopped and inquired about the health of their children.

We left McBride in the office with the manager and Tina took me out to the plant. The first thing I saw was people packing gold-painted matadors, toreadors and bulls into shipping crates the same as the ones I had seen on the stake truck outside. The processing area was divided into three separate sections and I could see that they were divided into bulls, toreadors and matadors.

"Actually," said Tina, "we should start at the other end, but I hate to pass that stinking rubber factory. Just follow me and watch where you put your feet."

The floor was covered with duckboards and about halfway along there was a clear plastic screen that didn't quite shield passersby from the water that was being sprayed. She walked me up the far end where pieces of lead, obviously pieces of salvaged scrap, were being loaded into a furnace. In front of the furnace there was the start of three conveyor chains and there were three buckets suspended from a gantry which came in turn to the furnace and were filled with molten lead.

As they were filled, the buckets moved over to the conveyor chains and started to fill the molds. The conveyor chain was in constant motion and as the filled molds traveled down the line they were replaced by empty molds from the underside of the chain. From where I stood I could see that it was only the bulls that were being sprayed with water; the matadors and toreadors went straight through without being sprayed.

I pointed that out to Tina and asked why. "Volume," she said. "We have these lines timed so that the toreadors and matadors are sufficiently cool when they reach the station where they are taken out of the molds. The bulls are slightly heavier and by the time they reach that part of the line they would be too hot to handle so we cool them off."

She showed me where they were sandblasted behind a heavy curtain to remove any sharp protuberances. From there they went, still on the conveyor chain, through what looked like a sea of gold paint then traveled under a bank of high-wattage light globes to the end of the line where they were taken off the conveyor and packed into the crates.

I looked in amazement. "Did you design all that?"

"It was my idea. I had a couple of engineers to work out the details."

"I'm very impressed." I picked up a bull and admired it.

"Sales are very brisk. Next to Spain, Mexico is *the* bullfighting country of the world."

"I'd like to take one of these with me."

"Sure, go ahead, take one of each."

"I'm afraid they would weigh too much, and I could hardly pin them on my lapel."

"Give your home address to Curtis and he'll see that you get one of each sent to your home address."

"You seem to have done a fantastic job here, but why do you dip them in the paint? I would have thought that the evaporation rate would just about empty the tank every day."

"We studied that and found that the evaporation rate over this area was considerably less than what we would lose if we sprayed them. And naturally, the labor costs preclude handpainting them."

"Even so, you must go through an enormous amount of paint."

"Let me show you." She led me to a side door, unlocked it and opened it to reveal a storage room piled from floor to ceiling with five-gallon containers of gold paint. "There is the bulk of our expenses. You know we get the lead practically for free, and right here is where we spend our money."

"Wouldn't it be cheaper to use black paint instead of gold?"

"There isn't that much difference in the price of paint, but the gold paint has more tourist appeal."

I tagged along behind her for a while; she visited the factory workers, stopping to talk to everyone. I had just seen a very different Tina from the champagne drinking brat. Not only was I impressed with her abilities as a factory designer, but I liked the way she talked to everyone who was working for her, something I had not seen at the mine. We finished the factory tour and went back into the office where we were served coffee; again I was struck by the rapport which Tina seemed to share with even the most junior members of the staff.

When Tina's attention was being held by the office workers, Curtis McBride leaned across to me and asked, "What did you think of it?"

"It showed me a side of her I never knew existed. Not only her abilities as a factory designer, but her relations with those people who have to work to make a living."

"Most of those people she has known for years," he told me. "She had this bright idea about making souvenir figurines and most of the people she hired at that time are still with her. She treats them very well. When any of their children are sick she has somebody send the kid a little gift. We have the best medical insurance in the country, and there is always a Christmas party for all the workers."

I said, "I didn't see the same rapport with the workers at the mine."

"Here she can wander around and talk to people, but she's bordering on the claustrophobic and she hates going into the mine. Besides which, miners live a solitary existence and any advance she made would be rejected."

"I can't imagine that."

"There is too much distinction. Miners prefer their reclusive lives and wouldn't know how to behave with a lady like Señora Rodriguez."

"And how do you get on with her?"

"I have my faults and she knows what they are, but she is willing to overlook them."

I was beginning to think that I had misjudged her. From what I had seen there in the foundry, McBride was not exaggerating. I had to hand it to her on the layout of the factory, and it was obvious that she had ideal relations with the workers. I hadn't noticed any claustropobic tendencies while she was down in the mine. What McBride had said about the miners preferring the solitary life may have been true, although it was not true of Cat Montez, who above anybody else would have chosen the solitary life over that of socializing. I consoled myself with the thought that I had given myself two choices: the first was Tina and my second was some of her staff. I didn't intend to wait much longer, I was carefully formulating plans to find out for sure that night.

Tina broke away from the group of office girls and joined McBride and myself over our coffee. McBride picked up a file and put it into his briefcase.

"Everything looks good," he said to Tina. "I'll turn these figures over to the accountants, but it looks pretty much the way we expected."

"In that case," said Tina, "we sould celebrate tonight. Curtis, have somebody reserve a table for six at that new nightclub. We'll go on the town tonight."

I really wasn't looking forward to the evening, but if I played my cards right I thought I could get away with it. When we arrived in the nightclub I wandered over to the bar where I slipped our waiter a thousand pesos and said, "Every time I order I'm going to ask for a martini.

That thousand is to make sure that you give me nothing but plain water."

"Oh, *si, señor*. I understand. There was another gentleman did that last week with his lady friend."

If he thought that I had nothing but rape on my mind that was fine as long as it worked. When I got back to the table Tina said, "What was that all about?"

I said, "Since we're celebrating I decided to change my order and drink martinis tonight."

"Very wise. I was wondering when you would get with it."

The toughest part was yet to come. As the rest of the party grew progressively more inebriated I had to match them with my slurred speech and uncoordinated muscles. I even danced with Gonsalez who had a very inviting body, but to do anything about it would be asking for trouble.

When we got back to the villa at two in the morning, my first reaction was to give up thanks that the chauffeur didn't drink, particularly in all that Mexican traffic.

On my way up to the bedroom I picked up a bottle of gin and one of vermouth. There was always a bucket of ice to cool Tina's champagne beside the bed and I mixed myself the first real martini of the day. After I got undressed I brought it over to the bed with a glass of fresh champagne for Tina. On my way I managed to slip the little white pill that I had palmed into the champagne. Everybody was already smashed and in less than five minutes Tina dropped the champagne glass and lay back on the bed. I quickly got dressed again and let myself out of the bedroom and down to the main entrance. I moved silently in case there were some members of the household staff still around. As far as the rest of the party was concerned I could have driven through there in a fire engine with all sirens blaring away and nobody would have heard me.

I ran, because I was not sure how much time I had at my disposal, for at least three miles out of the deserted residential area until I could get a cab. The driver was most reluctant to drive me into the industrial area, but money speaks every language. I had him drop me a block away from the foundry, picked the lock on the back door and let myself in.

The furnace was still warm and then I remembered that lead melts at about six hundred forty degrees Fahrenheit and that they would probably keep it warm overnight to prevent the excessive delay to bring it up to operating temperatures. I had no idea of what I was looking for; I had only thought of it when I saw so many gold figurines. I figured that if I browsed around long enough I would find some indication of Tina's guilt or innocence. The brief conversation I had had with McBride and seeing the way Tina behaved in the foundry had convinced me that my instincts had led me astray in this case, and that she might well be innocent of any wrongdoing. That wouldn't do the ghost of Dennis Gordon much good, but I had to take it into consideration.

I meandered around the conveyor chains and the work stations and through the carpenter's shop where they made the patterns for the molds. I even dipped my finger into the gold paint and got nothing for my trouble but a fingernail full of paint. I scrubbed at it with a tissue, but it was stubborn and I knew I could not appear at the villa with gold paint under my fingernail without arousing suspicion. I looked around for some solvent but I couldn't find any, then I thought of the paint storage room.

Tina had unlocked the padlock with a key that she had taken from her purse. When she was on such good terms with the workers that seemed an unnecessary precaution. I picked the padlock and went in the room to scrutinize the paint carefully. I pulled down one of the paint containers and pried the lid off. All it contained was gold paint in big streaks and I wondered how they mixed it up before pouring it into the paint trough.

There is a moment on every assignment when the truth hits hard. I went to the carpenter's shop and found myself a stick. Back in the paint storage room I dipped the stick into the paint until it hit bottom and then measured it against the side of the container. I had hit bottom at least three inches above where the bottom of the container should have been.

I put the stick down into the paint and scraped it across the bottom, but I couldn't dislodge anything. I finally had to roll up my sleeve and plunge my arm in and scrape it with Hugo. I found a sheet of newspaper and wiped Hugo, leaving behind what appeared to be a nugget of pure gold and a smearing of gold paint. I scraped again and stopped when I had about an ounce on the paper. I got a couple more sheets of paper and wrapped the gold with one of the bulls that I took from one of the crates then went back into the paint storage room and scrubbed my arm and hand with a paint solvent. That kind of stuff is not very good for the skin, and I hoped I had no cut on my finger or I would succumb to lead poisoning which would get me very little sympathy from Tina and her associates.

When I had scrubbed my hand and arm until I could see no sign of the paint, I returned the paint container, gathered up the bull, the paint and gold scrapings and let myself out, making sure I locked up behind me.

It was now four forty-five and I ran until I was able to find a cab. I gave him Butch Ramirez's address and when we arrived I emptied my pockets of loose *peso* notes and told him to wait for me on pain of death.

I rapped on the door and Butch eventually opened it clad in a tattered old bathrobe. I had known Butch Ramirez since he had worked with me on an assignment that involved the theft of a secret aluminum alloy and I always stopped by to see him whenever I was in Mexico City. He was one of the finest metallurgists in the world.

"Jesus Christ," he blurted, "you know what time it is?"

"You said stop by and see you anytime."

"Hey, Carter, is that really you?"

"In person, Butch. I don't have much time and I need a favor."

"Well, come on in. I'll make some coffee."

"No time for coffee. Grab this," and I thrust the bundle at him.

"What is it?"

"That's what I want you to tell me. There are what I believe to be scrapings of pure gold, some gold paint and a gold bull which I want you to analyze. Cable the results to David Hawk and I'll stop by and see you as soon as I get time."

"Sure, you can have it any time. I was about to get up anyway. It's five o'clock already."

"I'll see you later," I said. "I've got to get back before I'm missed."

I left him with the package clutched in his arms and ran down to the taxi. He let me out at the side of the villa where I climbed the wall and sneaked into the house. There was an aroma of fresh-perked coffee in the air and it was only minutes before the staff would be up and around busy with their chores. When I got to the bedroom Tina was still asleep. I took my clothes off, climbed into bed, spread her legs and penetrated her.

She opened her eyes and looked at me. "Nick, what are you doing?"

"I'm doing what I was trying to do last night when you fell asleep on me."

"In that case I missed out on it too. Let's make up for it."

EIGHT

A couple of hours later we got up and went down to the pool for our usual early morning swim and champagne and orange juice while the rest of the party slept on developing their hangovers. We had breakfast served and then Tina sent one of the servants to awaken Curtis McBride and have him meet her in the library.

Over a third cup of coffee she said, "Nick, I've got some business to take care of this morning which won't wait. Could you occupy yourself until lunch time? Would you like a tour of the city? I can have Willie Chan, Al or Carmen Gonsalez drive you around."

The thought of having one of them breathing down my neck repulsed me, and I could think of a couple of things I wanted to do that would cause comment had they known about it. I said, "If it's all the same I'd rather borrow a car and browse around."

"Sure, why not? There are several cars you can use, but don't take my Maserati; I'm kind of fussy about who drives it, it's my special baby. There are Cadillacs, Buicks and a Corvette you can have and I'll see you back here for lunch at noon."

I said, "Driving the Corvette might be fun. If you're sure you don't mind." Frankly I was surprised that she would let me out of her sight without somebody to spy on me. After breakfast I got dressed and went down to claim the Corvette from the chauffeur who was washing the Rolls; Tina went down to the library to wait for McBride.

I squealed the tires as I went down the driveway just to show that I was human and rejoiced in my luck. Being given the morning off meant that I could drive over to the embassy, call Hawk and then go in to see Butch Ramirez to find out what he could tell me about the gold and the bull.

I drove aimlessly around in the general direction of the city, then started to drive in the apparently haphazard pattern of somebody who is exploring the territory. Actually I was taking evasive action to make sure that I was not being followed. I was surprised that I was being allowed out alone and as soon as I was certain that I was not being tailed I pulled off to the side of the road and went over the Corvette looking for a bug. Either it was clean or I was slipping and couldn't find the obvious. I climbed back in and headed for the embassy.

I satisfied the marine guard as to my credentials, parked the car and went looking for the communications officer. I was seated at their scrambler set within minutes waiting for Hawk to answer my call. When it was answered it was Hugh Wilcox our communications officer who told me to wait while he got Hawk. But it wasn't Hawk who spoke to me but Debby, his secretary.

"Where's Mr. Hawk, Debby?"

"Oh, Mr. Carter, I'm so glad you called. I've just been talking to the President."

That sounded a little odd. Presidents talk to people like Hawk, they don't talk to secretaries. I had only spoken to him myself just once and that was an exception. "What's wrong, Debby?"

"Mr. Hawk has disappeared and the President wanted me to get in touch with you to try and find him."

"What happened?"

"He set off to arrange the security precautions for these peace talks, but his plane never arrived. The President is most upset and he asked me to contact you."

"I'll get there just as soon as I can. Keep all the information for me, so I can review it. I have no idea what time I can get a plane, but I'll be there sometime today. You can tell Mr. President that I'm on my way."

That must have devastated everyone's plans. As the senior operative under Hawk it was my responsibility to take over and form a task force to find Hawk. This meant that every operative would have to abandon his current assignment to concentrate on the search for Hawk. Whenever one of our operatives was killed, Hawk pulled all the stops and sent me or one of the other Killmasters out on the case. But for Hawk himself to become a casualty of executive action was unthinkable. No wonder the President was worried.

There was nothing I could do at the embassy but check the flight times out of Mexico City. In the States I would have commandeered a plane and left within the hour, but it would take too much time to unsnarl the red tape getting a USAF plane into Mexico City and out again. There was a flight at one o'clock which would get me into Miami in time for a flight that could bring me into Washington that evening.

I had plenty of time to catch the flight so I decided to go back to Tina's villa to make my excuses. My aunt had died or some similar reason. She was expecting me back at noon for lunch and that way I could return her car and start off with a clean slate. My thinking led me to my current assignment. I had enough time to stop by to see Butch Ramirez for a brief rundown on the bull and the gold. He could still cable the detailed report to Hawk, but this way I could wind it up before I left Mexico. If my suspicions were verified by Ramirez there would be a raid on the foundry by the customs and treasury officials and the Mexican police. There would be no further need for me. Hawk might insist that I take over some of the interrogation to get at who was responsible for Dennis Gordon's death, but my accountability would stop there.

The notion of finding Hawk and bringing him back to find my report sitting on his desk rather appealed to me. I had all too frequently been the target of Hawk's tongue-lashing when my idea of a reasonable schedule and his didn't match.

I walked downstairs and slid behind the wheel of the Corvette and drove over to Ramirez's place. Actually his name was Juan but the nickname of Butch had been tagged on in deference to his hair styling when most of us wore our hair down over our ears. He had changed his old bathrobe for a grubby shirt with the sleeves rolled up and a pair of work-stained jeans.

"Don't you ever sleep, Carter?" he greeted me.

"Sleep?" I asked. "What's that? Have you any information for me?"

"I can give you a brief summary on what you want to know, but the detailed report with the stuff like the specific gravity, melting points and actual purity is going to have to wait until this afternoon."

"Let's have it, Butch."

"The paint is a common lead oxide base, the kind of stuff you can buy in small quantities in any hardware store, but you don't want to hear about that."

"Tell me what I do want to hear about."

"The gold scraping is about ninety-seven fine which has been melted and recast again into its present form in a very crude furnace."

"What makes you say that, Butch?"

"The concentration of the impurities. You scraped that off the top, didn't you? If you had taken it off the bottom it would have told a different story."

"But even with the impurities it's still ninety-seven fine? How about the bull?"

"Oh, yes, the bull. The bull you will be *very* interested in. That bull is not lead, it's eighty-five percent lead and fifteen percent gold. There is not enough gold in it to change the color, which is why, if you break it or scrape it, it appears to be solid lead and it doesn't change the weight significantly."

"Have you still got the bull? I may need it for evidence."

"Most of it. I cut off a leg to analyze, and in the

process I destroyed it. I can still separate the gold from it though.''

"Keep it. Little enough payment for your trouble. I've been after a gang of gold smugglers. Once they get the bull over the border how difficult would it be to separate the gold?''

"Anybody with a basic knowledge of chemistry could do it with very crude equipment. And they would still have the lead to recast into bulls.''

"Thanks, Butch. That's all I needed to know.''

"You'll have to wait until this afternoon before I file my report. I am intending to write up the specific gravities and the properties of the lead/gold alloy. You might want to post them in all the customs offices for easy recognition.''

"Thanks very much, Butch. I'm indebted to you.''

"I knew you would be when I saw you on my doorstep at five o'clock in the morning.''

I stood up and ruffled his hair. It felt like my chin with a three-day growth of beard. "One of these days maybe I can repay you.''

"Stop by anytime—oh, I wish I hadn't said that. Stop by anytime during daylight hours.''

I went down to the Corvette and started driving back toward Tina's villa. I arrived there about eleven-thirty. I gave the Corvette to the chauffeur and as I walked up the front steps the door burst open and Tina ran down the steps to meet me. "I finished my meeting earlier than expected. Come in and have some lunch.''

"I'm sorry, Tina,'' I said. "There's been a change in plan. I'm afraid I can't stay. There was a message for me at the post office to call the family solicitor. My aunt has passed away and I have to return to Washington immediately. My aunt was my only living relative and I must take care of the legal matters and arrange for her funeral."

"Oh, that's too bad, Nick. Just as we were getting to know each other. Will you be back?"

"I have no idea. You know what these family lawyers are like. They might tie me up for months. And I'd hate to see the old duck shoved into any hole in the ground."

"Well come into the library for a farewell drink."

I had to pack my bag, but I figured I had enough time for a last drink with her. I was at a loss to explain the complete shift of attitude that I saw in her. For a while there she would not let me out of her sight unless somebody was standing beside me. Now she had accepted my excuses, offered to share a last drink with me and even seemed concerned about whether or not she would see me again. Maybe it was all this undying love bit that I expected momentarily, but Willie Chan would not play any part in that. If she was trying to convince me of her love it would have to be done in person. I'm sure Willie Chan had many good points, but I couldn't see him giving me a hard-on.

She led me into the library, ducked down and put a couple of highball glasses on top of the bar. I sauntered over and stood watching her across the bar. She bend down again and pulled out an ice tray. This was so unlike Tina to do the actual work herself it aroused my suspicions. Normally she would have called for one of the servants and given them the order. Perhaps it was all part of the plan to make a good impression on me.

She put a couple of ice cubes in each glass and then reached down and brought out a bottle of Gilbeys gin and a bottle of vermouth. Still suspicious I looked very closely at both bottles but I could see that neither of them had been opened. She opened the gin and poured about two ounces into each glass, splashed a little vermouth in, stirred them vigorously and handed one to me.

We touched glasses and I sipped a little of mine. She made a very strong martini. Tina came round the bar, took my arm and led me to a chair. I sipped again at my martini. "Well, I certainly hope to see you again soon, she said.

I tried to answer her, but nothing came out. This was ridiculous; I tried again without success. I heard a thunk and looked down to see my glass rolling on the floor where it had dropped from my fingers. That was even more ridiculous; I have perfect coordination of all my muscles. I wiggled my fingers but the message didn't get through to them. It was like looking at the fingers of a corpse. They just hung there lifeless. I put all of my psychophysical forces into play—the power that enables me to shatter four one-inch boards with a single blow of my fist—but to no avail. Tina came over to me and pushed me back in my chair.

She pulled up a footstool and sat there watching me. "Well, Mr. Carter. Now you know what it's like to be on the receiving end of a mickey. It really wasn't worthy of you to slip that pill to me last night. What was it? Chloral hydrate? Oh, that's right, you can't talk, can you?"

I tried anyway, but it didn't do me any good. "I hope

you didn't think that I would use anything that crude on you,'' she went on. ''I have a team of research scientists at my disposal, and one of my industries is the Rodriguez Pharmaceutical and Drug Company. We have been working on curare for a long time to get the utmost advantage from its paralyzing features. I hope I'm not boring you.'' She sipped at her martini.

''A long time ago my scientists came up with a form of curare in a colorless liquid that could be frozen. Since then I have kept a couple of ice cubes made of curare in the ice tray in the bar for just such an emergency as this.

''In case you didn't know it, curare is a drug that affects the motor muscles, which is why you can't move your arms or legs. It also paralyzes the throat and tongue which is why you can't articulate. It does not affect your sight and hearing. You can hear me, can't you? I can tell from the expression in your eyes that you can understand me.

''But to set your mind at rest, the dose I gave you will eventually wear off and you would get back to normal if there were no other plans for you. You'd like to know what those plans are, wouldn't you? But I'm not going to tell you. I had no intention of starting this for a few more days yet, but you forced my hand.

''It was extremely careless of you to slip me that knockout pill last night. Where did you go after I passed out? Back to the foundry? You were very interested in the gold, weren't you?

''You see, Mr. Carter, this has been planned for a long time and whatever you found out at the foundry just precipitated matters. We have been trying to get you into Central or South America for a long time. I thought that by smuggling gold over the border they would have sent you. But I was wrong. Even with all the money I spent sending that gold into your black market, you still didn't come. I finally had to kill off the guy they sent instead of you. That brought you running, didn't it? And if that hadn't worked, I kidnapped your boss.

"Yes, I have your David Hawk. You probably don't know that because you haven't been able to talk to your office yet. Or did you call them this morning? I've had him for two days. The only thing that AXE did wrong was to send you down here too soon after Gordon's death. I wasn't going to be ready for you for a couple more days. And then you jumped the gun by slipping me that knockout pill. I knew then that I couldn't stall it off any longer. No matter what you found out at the foundry, you forced my hand. I had to give you your freedom so that you would seem to be following up on your assignment so that nothing would appear to be out of place."

She leaned over me and I could see her hand come up to my eye. "You're still awake and listening, I see."

I tried to say something to show her that I was still in charge of the situation, but it came out garbled, like the ramblings of a mental patient. Tina had told me that it was a very mild dose she had given me, so I consoled myself with what I would tell her when I recovered my speech. It was the first time I had been on the receiving end of something like that, and I didn't like it very much.

Tina had apparently had her say and I was making all

the conversation of a boiled cabbage. She got up and drank from her martini, set the glass on the bar and left the room. I went to work on my body straining to move it by sheer willpower. The only thing I could move were my eyes and, since I was sitting with my back to the door, they weren't able to tell me much. When she came back into the room I had no knowledge of her presence until she appeared before me. For all I know she might have been standing out of sight behind my chair. Except that Al and Willie Chan were with her. I had never been exactly overjoyed to see either of them and this was no time to change my opinion. When I saw that Al was carrying a hypodermic syringe I was even less enthusiastic than before.

Willie Chan grabbed me by the front of my shirt and pulled me upright while Al made amends for all the humiliation I had caused him. He thrust the hypodermic in with such force I expected to see the point break through on the other side of my arm. Willie Chan let me go and I dropped into the chair again. I tried to fight off the waves of blackness that surrounded me. For a while there I had it beaten, but the tide of blackness kept getting larger until it swamped me and even my eyesight and my hearing failed me.

NINE

I had no idea of how long I had been lying here, so I made sure my arms and legs were working properly and starting doing some calisthenics in order to get the blood flowing freely. Once I started feeling human again I began to explore my surroundings. I couldn't see what I was walking on, so I found it more expedient to walk on all fours.

The floor seemed reasonably flat but covered with small rocks. I picked up a handful and started throwing them around me waiting to hear one of them bounce off a wall. Admittedly they were small rocks, but all I heard was the rattle of them on the floor a long way from me. I went through my pockets to find that I had lost Wilhelmina and Hugo, not very surprising under the circumstances. Everything else seemed to be in order. I still had my passport, my cigarette case and a butane lighter. I also had a pocketful of loose change, my wallet and my keys, and much to my surprise I still had Pierre strapped to the inside of my thigh. Pierre has saved my life innumerable times, and I was thinking that this just might be another one. I lit a cigarette and meditated on the situation.

Before my cigarette lighter died out I took a look around and could see nothing at all. There were no walls or obstacles on the floor. I felt much the same as an ant dropped in the middle of the Sahara desert. Somewhere there must be an end to all this nothingness, a wall, a person, a piece of machinery. Anything to tell me that I was not all alone here; best of all, there must be a way out of here, some contact with civilization.

Since I had not been able to see any walls or hit them with the rocks I threw, I thought this might be the start of a brainwashing process that begins by completely disorienting the victim. If this were the case, I was determined to meet my captors on my own two feet. I stubbed out my cigarette, rose to my feet and began to walk in as straight a line as the rocks underfoot would allow. I often stumbled when a rock overturned beneath my foot, but I encountered no walls, obstacles or pits. I just trudged along wearily. I knew I was not in the open air because of the lack of stars and the moon. Also the air surrounding me was stagnant, so I knew I was in an enclosed space; but I couldn't for the life of me figure what it could be. If it had been turf underfoot I might have thought it was an enclosed football field. I had no idea how long I walked in this fashion before I finally saw a light.

It was a diffused light, as though it came from a single source beyond a wall and was reflected from several screens. No matter what it was, it was the first sign of life I had seen since I had recovered consciousness and I headed toward it. As I drew closer I could see that it came from an open door. The light was not directly in line with the door but was being shielded from it by some kind of a screen.

I hurried my steps toward it and when I reached it I found it to be only about three feet wide. I could see that the light came from an artificial screen about twenty feet away across the rock-strewn floor. I stepped through the gap and as I did so a blanket dropped over my head effectively blinding me.

The blanket was held by two strong men, and unable to see, my struggles were in vain. They quickly shackled my hands behind me with handcuffs and carried me away. I thought I was being treated to a taste of what had been planned for me in the goldsmithing area in Montevideo, or had I succumbed to the attackers at the mine. They carried me easily. I could see brief flashes of light seeping under the blanket where it had been tied down over my head, so apparently I was the only one working in the dark. I could tell from the constant shift of directions that they were not carrying me in a straight line, but more like through the various rooms of a house.

Without warning I was suddenly dropped and somebody knelt beside me and unlocked the handcuffs. I tore at the blanket that had so successfully blinded me, but I was not fast enough. By the time I had rid myself of it, the men were gone and I just saw a door closing over the light of what was probably a kerosene lantern. There was still the stagnant smell about the air but I was not in a large space this time.

I flicked my cigarette lighter and I could see that I was in an enclosed room about ten feet square. I went over to the door but it had been fastened from the outside. The floor and the walls were of rough-hewn stone and there were no windows. I lit a cigarette and contemplated my position.

My captors seemed intent on not letting me know where I was or with whom I was dealing. Apparently Tina was the mastermind behind the whole thing, and from what she had said there were plans to use me. That left me with a choice: she could either kill me and leave my body where it would embarrass the most people—like the Russian embassy—or use me as a hostage. If she had any idea of using me as a hostage she could forget it; I've seen Hawk throw away good men when it suited his purpose but it did have one consideration. If they intended to keep me alive they would have to feed me. Over the last few days I had eaten extremely well, but not so well that I would take kindly to being starved.

I had been squatting there on my heels trying to make sense out of this whole business when the door opened and somebody was thrust in beside me. The figure lay there on the ground and started to groan. I reached down and turned the person over, then lit my cigarette lighter.

It was David Hawk and he was a mess. His face was black and blue, one eye was completely closed and he had a welt such as is caused by a blow from a pistol barrel running from his left ear to his jaw. His shirt was ripped open and his entire chest was covered with bruises. There was no water available to clean him up. I cradled his head in my arm and he kept groaning. I lit a cigarette and he opened his good eye and looked at me.

The groaning stopped and he said, "When are you going to learn to appreciate a good cigar, Carter?"

I put the cigarette in his mouth. "For all the noise you were making I thought you were dead."

"Just acting, Carter."

"I'm the only audience you have now so you can give it up. What happened to you?"

"I just got a taste of what I've been warning you guys about for years."

I was tempted to observe that he had come out of the encounter second best, but I waited for him to tell me about it.

"For Christ's sake. Why the hell do a bunch of hoods think that pounding on a man's ribs and face is going to make him tell everything that he knows?"

"What were they trying to find out?"

"None of your business, Carter."

I resented that until I realized that neither of us had checked the room for a bug. "Let's get you cleaned up first," I said, "and then we can talk."

I walked over to the door and pounded on it with my clenched fist. I thought that we had been abandoned and that everybody had left us to our misery. But it was not likely that they would have given up on David Hawk without trying to get the same information out of me.

After several minutes of incessant pounding I heard a shuffling noise outside the door. A peephole was opened and the light that came in was promptly blocked by a bloodshot eye. "What have you done to Mr. Hawk?" I demanded. "He needs a doctor."

The voice that answered me was that of an uneducated Central or South American. The type of accent that one might find among the lower classes, perhaps belonging to a miner or a foundry worker. "There is no doctor here."

"Then we must get him to a hospital. He has several broken ribs. I demand that you take him to a doctor."

"You are in no position to demand anything. Shut up and don't make so much noise."

I wasn't about to give up now that I had his attention. I jabbed at the eye with my forefinger but it backfired on me. He grabbed my finger and the next moment was clamping his teeth into it. He pulled his head back from the peephole and I could see an unshaven face with a set of broken, yellowed teeth. "If you can't get him to a doctor, give me some light and some water so that I can clean him up to see the extent of the damage and see what I can do for him." He let go of my finger and slammed the peephole almost catching my finger. I went back to Hawk and squatted beside him.

"That was just about what I expected," he said.

"You didn't see the teeth he bit me with. If I was a gambling man I'd lay odds that I have rabies." I leaned forward and found Hawk's ear in case the place was bugged. "Who are they and what do they want?"

"They're a bunch of cutthroats, and I don't know what they want. How did you get here?"

"I came first class all the way, I said. "I am the privileged guest of Señora Tina Rodriguez."

"Carter," Hawk told me, "I knew you would get into trouble with all that sleeping around."

"I wasn't sleeping around, I was merely trying to establish a rapport with my main suspect."

"Well, what have you found out about her?"

"She is the one who has been responsible for the gold smuggling. They're using an alloy of eighty-five percent lead and fifteen percent gold to slip it over the border where the gold is separated, and the lead is recast into more figurines or battery plates or what-have-you. There will be a report on your desk when you get back."

"It's a pity you didn't decide to carry it back yourself."

"I would have tried," I told him, "but Rodriguez has a handy little paralyzing drug that comes in the form of an ice cube."

I had barely finished speaking when the door opened and two men came in. The first stood with his back to the wall and covered us with an Ingram M10 submachine gun while the other set down a pail of water, a grubby towel and a stub of candle.

I looked more closely at the man who was holding the Ingram. If it had been a pistol that he was holding so carelessly, or even a shotgun I would have chanced jumping him, but I will not mess with an Ingram M10 in an enclosed space. Those little monsters spew out slugs at the phenomenal rate of twenty per second. The most coordinated of hands have trouble keeping a burst down to one and a half second which will empty a thirty-two shot magazine and I had no desire to be in the same room as an itchy trigger finger holding one of those.

I decided to wait and make a break for it later on when our guards were equipped with some less frightening armament. The men backed out of the door, slammed it and replaced the bar that locked it.

Turning my attention to my patient, I lit the candle with my cigarette lighter then dampened the towel and put it over Hawk's closed eye. He started groaning again. "The guards have gone," I told him. "There's no need to act."

"Who's acting? Florence Nightingale you ain't, Carter."

"You shouldn't have got yourself so messed up. I hope you've got medical insurance, this is only a temporary job to enable you to help me get you out of here."

"What do you think I pay you for, Carter? Go ahead and get us out. You don't need to wait for me. I can keep up with you."

"The next time they come back," I promised him.

It was a very short-lived promise. I set to work to bathe the worst of his bruises and checked his ribs out. Apparently there was nothing broken, except my promise. Within a few minutes the door opened and this time there were three men. Two of them carried Ingrams and had Colt .45 automatics strapped to their waists. If I was too sensible to make a break under the watchful eye of one Ingram, I was doubly so when there were two of them. The man who had carried in the water earlier seemed to be in charge and he motioned to us to follow him while the other two brought up the rear.

I was puzzled as to where we were. The enormous area in which I had recovered consciousness, the small, cell-like room I had been tossed into with David Hawk and now this dimly lit passageway all spoke of primitive subterranean accommodations carved out of solid rock. I could not think of any place where such a solid mass of rock was indigenous, and I had no chance to discuss the matter with Hawk. It was obvious that we were being taken to be interviewed by somebody, and I hoped to be able to get the answer from him.

TEN

When we reached the end of the passageway we went through an open door into a large room which looked as though it had been designed as a banquet hall for some medieval king. The room was at least fifty feet long and half that wide. At the far end, seated on a ridiculously anachronistic aluminum framed chair, was a very large man wearing a green baseball cap, a pair of very bushy eyebrows and a beard that reached halfway to his waist. Between that and the hot breath of the guard behind me I felt as though I was being watched from the depths of the Vietnamese jungle. The lighting was supplied by torches in holders around the walls which not only gave us a good look at him, but at his supporters who were ranged round the walls squatting on their heels. They all wore the same kind of green baseball cap, but their clothing ranged from bare feet through sandals to army style boots and from ragged jeans and equally tattered shirts to serapes. Each one of them was holding an Ingram M10 and I saw several Colts stuck in belts.

We were brought up to face the bearded man who glared at us from over the hirsute growth. He fondled his beard and I was surprised not to see a few bats flying out of it. "Have you decided to talk yet, Hawk?" He spoke an educated Spanish which probably meant that he was a member of a terrorist band from some Central or South American country.

Hawk spoke with all the patience he would have shown a three-year-old child. "I have already told you that I didn't know my destination. I had orders to complete the security arrangements for the peace talks. I would have known where they were to be held if your idiotic rebels hadn't decided to hijack the plane and kill off the crew."

"What about you, Carter? What can you tell us?"

"I haven't heard the question yet."

"What peace talks are those? The ones between Russia and America, the ones between Israel and Egypt, or between Iran and Iraq?"

"Don't try to fool me."

"I've been busy. I haven't read a paper for two weeks. I can't be expected to keep track of all the uprisings in every two-bit nation."

He made a motion and I could hear an Ingram being cocked behind me. That is as blood-chilling a sound as I have ever heard.

"We are not speaking of any two-bit nation. I am speaking of Peru. Don't tell me you haven't heard about the move by Peru, Colombia and Ecuador to take over Panama?"

"I can't understand why they would want to."

"You can't be as stupid as you appear. The Panama

Canal is a constant source of revenue to whoever holds it. One of the largest natural resources in the Americas."

"Are you telling me that you and this unwashed team of louts are going to take over Panama?"

"It has all been done officially. We are the Children of the Revolution. We approached our respective governments to make an offer to Panama to form a union of the countries such as was done with the United States of America. I need to know where the peace talks are to be held."

"If there is no war, there would not be any point to having peace talks."

"When our respective governments turned down our request to form a union with Panama we, the Children of the Revolution, decided to take action."

"Don't tell me that you are going to change the course of the world before you take over your own governments."

"For my part, and those of my fellow South Americans anywhere, there has not been a satisfactory government since the days of Juan Perón in Argentina."

"I still think you would do better to take over your own government first. The government of any nation is not going to listen to anybody who does not have the authority of leadership."

"They will listen to us, I can assure you. Now where were the peace talks to be held?"

I said, "You still haven't convinced me that there is any need for peace talks."

"I am not in the mood to try to convince you of anything. Where are the talks to be held?"

I looked at Hawk but received no signal from him. "I'm hungry," I told the bearded man. "If you are intending to carry on this pointless conversation the least you can do is feed us."

"A typical American reaction. The only thing on your mind is your own personal comfort. You don't care about the deprivations that are being caused to your fellow men."

I turned to Hawk. "Are you hungry, sir?"

"These bastards don't intend to feed us. I think we'd better get out of here before we starve."

"For your information," we were told, "preparations are being made to feed you."

"I didn't think there were any fast-food chains in Panama."

"Who said anything about Panama. We're in Peru."

I said, "And you think that the Panamanian government is going to send representatives all the way to Peru to negotiate with a bunch of cutthroat rebels."

"If you recall, I was trying to find out where the talks were to be held."

"I don't think you talk is very peaceable, and I'm sure that if anybody had been paying attention that neither Mr. Hawk or myself have any idea of where the talks are to be held. If you're contemplating busting a few more ribs to find out what we have already told you, have at it."

He clapped his hands in true King Arthur sytle and said, "Take them away and feed them."

We were grabbed by the guards and led away down the passage to another cell-like room. This one was furnished with a little more comfort. There was a crude table with two benches pulled up to it and an assortment of food on top. There was the usual pail of water, a couple of grubby towels, a sliver of soap, a couple of disposable razors, probably from my baggage, and a couple of toothbrushes. The room was lighted by the usual torches held in clamps around the walls which seemed to be the standard for lighting in this area.

When our guards withdrew and locked the door behind them the first thing that Hawk and I did without conferring was to go over the entire room for hidden microphones. It was similar to the one we had been in before and it took us very little time to assure ourselves that they had not set up any bugging devices.

"Well, at any rate, we're free to talk," said Hawk.

"You start in," I said. "What's all this about peace talks?"

"As you realize, America has a vested interest in the Panama Canal. And like the man said it is the only natural resource of Central America. A constant source of revenue to whoever holds it. Apparently there were three independently formed groups of rebels, these Children of the Revolution who felt that their governments should take over the canal. These three groups all kidnapped a high official from their own government—one from Peru, one from Colombia, one from Ecuador—and insisted that they go to war to seize Panama and control the canal. Naturally, the governments declined and the Children of the Revolution decided that they would do it themselves without the blessing of the government.

"This thing escalated to such a pitch that the United States had to step in with the permission of the United

Nations to organize peace talks between the four nations, or at least three bands of rebels and one official government."

"And where did you come in, sir?" I asked.

"I was charged with the security of the peace talks. It's bad enough trying to police talks between three different nations, but can you imagine what bad feelings must be aroused by three different bands of rebels?"

"Then you do know where the peace talks are to be held."

"That information was given to representatives of the governments that will attend the talks. I have no intention of giving it to a bunch of unwashed rebels whose motives are definitely suspect. They tell us we're in Peru, so presumably they are on their own home ground. Giving that information to a bunch of rebels from Peru might lead to an attack on the officials of Panama, Colombia, Ecuador or even their own country."

I gestured toward the table with the food. "Let's make ourselves at home, unless you think that might be poisoned."

"I think we can eat all we want without fear of being poisoned."

I sat down at the table, broke off a length of freshly baked bread, picked up a chunk of goat's cheese and started munching. "Tina Rodriguez said something about having a use for me. Do you think she meant this business?"

Hawk was eating a crudely made cheese sandwich. "Figure it out for yourself, Carter. If you and I were to be found dead at the scene of a successful assassination attempt on one of these official heads of government there would be a thorough investigation and America would be held responsible. If our bodies showed up unshaven and half starved nobody would believe it and would see through it as an attempt to discredit America in some South American squabble."

I said, "I'm not about to starve the body which has given me such good service just to point an accusing finger at a bunch of rebels. Pass the cheese, sir."

I finished off the cheese and started to peel a banana. "Then the only thing we can possibly do is to escape. Actually I had that in mind all along."

Hawk said, "We must escape and uncover the attempt that will be made on some official's life, and show it for what it is."

"If we are to believe them," I pointed out, "we are in Peru. Does that mean that we're close enough to the peace talks for us to postpone them until we have uncovered this assassination attempt?"

"Peru is one hell of a big country," said Hawk. "It all depends on where in Peru we are, and where the peace talks will be held."

"I thought you knew."

"There is no reason why the location should not have been changed when I was reported missing. Do you have any idea where we might be?"

"From what I have seen of the place it's a gigantic conglomeration of caves, which to my knowledge doesn't exist in Peru. Either that or we are in one of the Inca's points of civilization."

"Sir," I went on, "Tina Rodriguez said that she and her colleagues had been trying to get me into Central

America for a long time. Is it possible that their plans to assassinate some official have been in limbo for that long?"

"The Children of the Revolution was formed about six months ago."

"In that case it might have been formed with that idea in mind. Try this theory on for size and see if it fits all the facts. Suppose Tina and that bearded monstrosity out there didn't like the current Peruvian government. Perhaps Tina had a falling out with the president: they are both extremely powerful people and despite Tina's millions she could have upset *El Presidente* and was sent into political exile. All of her millions would not do her any good unless she could overthrow the government and set herself up as a candidate for that office. After Evita Perón's length of time in office in Argentina the Peruvians would probably not be sexist and she would have a good chance. All she would have to do would be to make arrangements to have Hernando Martinez assassinated and she could then run for office. Power is always at the top of the list of motives even surpassing money and sex. How does that sound to you, sir?"

Hawk helped himself to one of my cigarettes, but his expression denied that he would get much enjoyment from it. "It certainly could fit all the existing facts as we know them, but where does the gold come in?"

"According to Tina, they started to smuggle the gold into the States not so much to undermine our economy but to lure me into Central or South America. They had a setback when you sent Dennis Gordon down here, but they killed two birds with one stone—you should excuse the expression—when they got rid of him in such a way that you would be forced to send me or one of the other Killmasters. Tina admitted that the gold smuggling had cost her plenty but when power is the motivating force I guess money is no object."

"Where did they get all that gold, Carter?"

"Gold is mined along with lead and she has several lead mines in Peru. She actually took me to one of her lead mines in Uruguay. Unfortunately there is no gold to be mined in Uruguay, it all comes from Peru. Maybe she thought that if I saw it actually being mined I might have stumbled on the answer a lot sooner. As it was she could have shown me all the gold she mined and I would never have connected it with an assassination attempt on the President."

"Do you think they mined all the gold that has been flowing in the States?"

"I have no idea of the quantities we are talking about, but she must have; either that or she found the secret of the fairy tales, like the goose that laid the golden egg."

"You're letting your imagination run away with you, Carter. Get your mind back to the present. How do we get out of here?"

"Leave that to me, sir. I'll jump the guards and get us out of here."

"And then what will you do? You don't have any idea of where we are."

"We have been told that we're in Peru. If this isn't a labyrinth of caves, and I don't think it is, it must be one of the Inca's points of civilization which means that we must be up in the mountains somewhere. So all we have to do is to head for the sea. As long as we head west we'll get there and if it's any consolation it'll be downhill all the way."

Hawk said, "I get the feeling from the way you're avoiding the subject that you don't know anything about these Inca points of civilization."

"I don't, sir, but then neither does anybody else. There are a number of these buildings which are easily recognizable by the traditional trapezoidal shape of the blocks that were used by the Incas. So little is known about the civilization that nobody knows whether they were built as fortresses, temples, seats of learning or communal centers for the villages. Personally I tend to the theory that they were temples, which would explain the enormous size of some of the rooms and the small cells which would have housed the monks or priests in residence. On the contrary, the Incas were sun-worshippers and I find it difficult to explain why they would build a structure that closed out the sun."

Hawk said, "Let's get the hell out of here, we can theorize all we want back in my office."

I walked over to the pail of watcr, dunked a tooth-brush and scrubbed at my teeth. Next I dampened my face and tried to get a lather out of the sliver of soap we had been left and tugged away at my beard. It wasn't the closest shave I've ever had, but it made me feel more human. To put my morale back to where it should be I needed a shower but I thought that Hawk was showing signs of impatience and I was reluctant to ask him to pour the rest of the water over me. Anyway he may have been considering brushing his own teeth.

When I was finished I squatted down on my heels, dunked the towel and scrubbed at my face.

I was right about Hawk's dwindling patience. "If you're quite satisfied with your appearance, Carter, let's get on with it."

"Everything is going to plan," I told him. "We're waiting for somebody to come and unlock the door for us."

Although I had not seen any, I knew that somebody would be in to clear away the remnants of the food before rats could get a foothold on the place.

We didn't have long to wait. Within ten minutes I heard the sound of the bar being removed from the outside of the door. It opened and a guard came in and stood with his back to the wall aiming the Ingram at a point on the floor between Hawk and myself. Another guard came in and started to stack the dishes.

I dabbed at my face with the damp towel and said, "You'd better get that out of here. That's enough to poison a man."

"Don't you like goat's cheese?" From the way he spoke they must have been planning on leaving our cleaned up well-fed carcasses at the scene of the assassination.

"I like goat's cheese," I told him, "but that bread is moldy."

"That bread was baked yesterday."

"You can see the mildew on it." I sauntered over to the table and picked up a crust of bread. "Look, you can see it right there."

He took the crust in his hand and peered at it.

"Where? I don't see it."

I took the crust from his hand. "Right there. Are you blind?"

I turned toward the armed guard and held the crust out to him. "Surely you can see that. It's mildew."

As he stepped forward, I dropped the crust of bread and snapped the towel at his eyes, then lashed out at his neck with the edge of my hand. He crumpled up in a heap on the floor and I grabbed the Ingram and covered the other guy.

He stood back against the wall with his hands raised. I took the Colt from the guard's belt, came forward and slammed the barrel down on the man's head. He subsided gently onto the floor and Hawk and I made for the door.

There was nobody waiting outside so we stepped out and closed the door, replacing the bar that effectively locked them in. Although I had no idea of where we were in the compound, I had no wish to revisit the scene of our last interview so I headed off in the opposite direction. It grew progressively darker and very soon we had reached the utmost limits of the light. I stopped and took a couple of torches from their holders and handed one to Hawk who was treading on my heels.

The place seemed to form a circle around the arena where I had first recovered consciousness. When we found ourselves there I lit my torch and led the way round the walls. It was not much more effective than the stumbling around in the dark I had first done, but it showed that there were doorways at intervals of twenty feet or so. Since most of these openings were blocked by fallen masonry I was quickly assured that we had been moving in the wrong direction, and that the only route to freedom was to go back past the obviously inhabited section. However, I'm a stubborn cuss and I kept going looking for an unblocked passage. Finally by my reckoning we had completed a complete circuit when we heard voices.

They spoke Spanish but were not close enough for me to understand what they said and the voices had all the eerie quality of an echo chamber. I put the Ingram on automatic fire and snicked off the safety catch. At an automatic rate of twenty shots per second I would have done much better to put it on single shot and conserve my ammunition, but the Ingram has no sights, just a five-inch barrel which goes into a cloth-bound silencer to protect the user's hands from the scorching heat. In the flickering torchlight I could not take aim and hoped that one quick burst of maybe half a second would bring all the discouragement we needed to give us an opportunity to escape.

I pushed Hawk away from me and was gratified to see him lie face down. I stood my ground with my left side pointing forward to the enemy and the Ingram tucked under my right arm. Our pursuers saw us and several of them raised their guns. I heard the silenced stammer and a volley of bullets passed over my head. I aimed low, knowing how the Ingram creeps up on automatic fire, and squeezed off a half-second burst. There are silencers and silencers, but I have never heard one so efficient as the one I was holding. The goddamned magazine was empty.

I threw it aside and snatched out the Colt. I cocked it and squeezed off the first shot. Nothing happened. It sometimes happens that the first round in a Colt will jam so I cocked it again to free the offending shell and bring the next one into the firing chamber. Again I squeezed off the trigger and again nothing happened.

Disgusted I threw the Colt at our pursuers and put my hands over my head and started to walk toward them with Hawk following. Hawk had seen the whole thing which was just as well because I would have been acutely embarrassed to recount my aborted escape attempt.

ELEVEN

Hawk and I were shepherded through the compound with a pack of snapping, snarling human sheep dogs at our heels. I took notice of our route now that I had the light of the torches and it seemed to me that it was the only passageway in use and ran from the arena to the banquet room where we had been interviewed. Several of the doors to the small rooms were open, apparently where the guards had been called out to give chase to us.

When we got to the banquet room the bearded man was seated in his aluminum-frame chair, but I noticed that it was not in the exact spot it had been before. He too had been called from his room and had taken the chair with him. That set me to wondering how the alarm had been set off. There was no way our original guards could have warned the others except by banging on the door which had not been of much use when I had tried it earlier.

Once again we were deposited at the feet of the chief while the hangers-on ranged themselves around the walls.

"So you don't like our bread, Carter."

"Actually I like it very much, it's you and your associates I don't like which was why I was trying to widen the distance between us."

"I had been told that you were tricky; that's why your guard was armed with an unloaded gun. It paid off for me."

"If it hadn't been for that you might have had less followers."

"The number of disciples one has is a reflection of the popularity of the cause."

"Do you mean to tell me that every one of these louts is interested in who controls the Panama Canal?"

"Not *per se*. They are interested in the wealth that comes with their being part of the richest nation in the Americas."

"I think you would have gained more popularity by distributing the gold than by smuggling it over the border."

"Easy come, easy go. Our smuggling served its purpose. It brought you and your friend into our control."

"I've seen how hard these miners work, and if that's what you call easy come, you can have it."

"Did you actually believe that all the gold that was being smuggled to undermine the economy of the United States came out of the ground?"

"Where else could it have come from?"

"I suppose you're right in one sense. That is the gold

I used to buy an equal partnership with Señora Rodriguez."

"You don't look like the kind of person who would have inherited wealth. You look more like a dunghill keeper," I commented.

"I am a mining engineer, and it was I who found all the gold."

"You should have bought a clean shirt. You don't look like the kind of person who would do any honest labor. So it was you who mined the gold, was it?"

"I didn't mine it."

"But you just said that it came out of the ground."

"Let's just say that I recovered it. Several people came to Peru in 1945 and wanted to make a trip into the interior up into the Andes. My father was one of the guides they hired. One night two of the people slipped out of the camp and buried a trunk. My father took note of the spot and made a map. After that, they lost enthusiasm for their trip and returned to Lima. My father died in an auto accident a couple of years later without having had the chance to revisit the spot. I found the map in his belongings and as soon as I had finished school and started practicing my profession I started looking for an opportunity to go look for it."

"What did you find? The fabulous treasure of the Incas?"

"No, much better than that. I found the chest. When I opened it there were a number of documents that had been destroyed by the damp and a couple of armbands with swastikas on them. I had found one of the Nazis' treasure hoards."

By now I was fascinated by the tale. "And you carried it down out of the mountains?"

He looked at me with contempt. "Do you have any idea of how much gold weighs, Carter? I reburied it where I could find it easily and brought one ingot back with me on my mule. Since then I have made several trips into the mountains each time bringing back two ingots."

"That should have kept you in comfort for the rest of your life."

"It was a temptation. I tried the life of luxury but there was something missing. I wanted power and it was at that time that Señora Rodriguez had been trying to replace our president. She failed and tried to overthrow the government with a rebellion. I went to see her and offered my wealth to help her overthrow the existing cabinet, in exchange for a position of responsibility in the new government."

"And she accepted your offer?"

"When the rebellion failed, Señora Rodriguez was exiled and does not dare to show her face in Peru again. I am her representative in Peru and when we get rid of Hernando Martinez and put Tina Rodriguez into power I shall be the new vice president."

"Then what was all that talk about Panama?"

"The Panama Canal is still the world's largest natural resource, but we could hardly walk in there and take the canal away and put it in Peru. In order to make it work we need the support of Colombia and Ecuador. They are poor nations and as such are greedy; they were only too willing to go along with our plans."

"I still don't think you have any chance of convincing the United Nations."

"Why not? When Hernando Martinez is found there will be indisputable evidence that it was the work of the United States of America. We shall have all the world on our side."

That pretty well confirmed the suspicions of Hawk and myself that made it even more imperative that we escape. I had one final question for him.

"When does all this take place?"

"Not for for two more days yet. Are you that anxious to die?"

"Who said that I was going to die?"

"I say so, and if you have any questions it was the decision of the Children of the Revolution."

"I am very impressed," I said sarcastically.

He leaned back in his chair and toyed with his beard. "So, Carter, you've tricked me again. I had absolutely no intention of giving you all that information, but you deceived me."

"It's my childlike innocence," I said. "That's what does it every time."

"I can equate childlike with your naïvete, but I could not call you innocent. You will be taken back to your room and this time there will be two guards, both of whom will have loaded guns. And if either of them allows you to escape he will be put to death."

"Suppose they both allow me to escape?"

"Then they will both be killed."

"Then I hope you've got plenty of guards."

He gestured imperiously and two guards came forward and pushed Hawk and I back to the room we had occupied before at the point of a brace of Ingrams.

Somebody had been in the room since we had left. The table had been cleared, a couple of canvas cots had been left there and the pail had been refilled with water. I didn't like that very much: it made them far too confident that we would be staying. And, as if to underline that fact both guards lifted their weapons and fired a short burst over our heads.

It is impossible to count the number of shots at twenty per second, and the Ingram silencer is one of the most effective I have ever seen. When the guards left I looked at the wall over our heads and found eleven bullet holes which meant that both of them had been able to conttrol the burst to quarter a second, no mean feat when the damned thing jumps around so much. I immediately decided not to give the guards a chance to shoot at us when we broke out of there.

When they had gone Hawk and I turned to each other. "What next, Carter?"

I said, "Let's just call the last one practice. We've found which way not to go. So now we have to break out and go the other way, through the room where we were interviewed."

"And just how are we going to do that?"

"I won't say it's easy but we can do it. How long can you hold your breath, sir?"

"Probably about a minute and a quarter or a minute and a half. Are you thinking what I think you're thinking?"

"Let's give it a try just to see. I don't want to kill you trying."

Hawk nodded and watched me. I looked at my watch and as the sweep hand passed the twelve I pointed my finger at him. He took a deep breath and held it. He certainly did very well and didn't release his breath until he had gone red in the face and was obviously suffering considerable discomfort. He finally let go of it with a whooshing noise, and immediately his chest started pounding until he got back to normal again.

I looked at my watch. "One minute twenty-five seconds. I'm afraid that just won't do, sir. That stuff lasts for two minutes. I can hold my breath for three minutes, but in a confined space like this it may last longer than the usual two minutes."

Hawk squatted on his heels with his back to the wall, and I went over and sat beside him and gave him a cigarette. "What now?" he asked.

"I'm afraid I'm fresh out of ideas," I said. "You can't last the distance if I release Pierre and the guards have demonstrated that they have loaded guns and are not averse to using them."

He dragged deep on his cigarette. "Let's look at it another way. What would you do if you were here alone?"

"Well, knowing how ready the guards are to shoot, I would make some kind of disturbance and when the guards came rushing in I would release the gas in Pierre. When they had succumbed I would help myself to a submachine gun and an automatic and walk out of here."

"Wouldn't you be afraid of getting caught again?"

"When they brought us back again I noticed that most of the doors were open where the guards had rushed out, so from that I figured it must be night and that everybody is sleeping. If I was very quiet I could probably sneak out unnoticed."

Hawk said, "That is exactly what I want you to do now."

I looked at him waiting for the words to sink in. "I can't do that, sir."

"Why the hell not?"

"For several reasons. One, I couldn't just walk out on you. Second, I don't know where the peace talks are to be held. And third, I told Debby to tell the President that I would find you and bring you back."

"The peace talks are being held on an aircraft carrier, the *U.S. Abraham Lincoln*. When you get there I want you to take charge of the security arrangements and see if you can put a stop to this assassination attempt on President Martinez."

"Sir, I can't just walk out and leave you."

"Are you afraid of what the President will say to you?"

I have known and respected David Hawk for several years and even though a bawling out from the President of my country was something I would not look forward to, there was another reason. But how can you tell the man who has trusted you and trained you to operate with a lack of emotion about compassion.

"Let's just say that I can't do it, and leave it at that."

"Carter," said Hawk, "we have been together for quite a while and during that time you have often seen me send a man out knowing that he was going to get killed."

"Yes, sir. Benny Chang was one and more recently Dennis Gordon."

"Do you think I like doing that?"

"I'm quite sure you didn't, but it was your job."

"Exactly, and it is your job to complete this assignment."

I said, "This is probably the most difficult thing you have ever asked me to do."

"Carter, I'm not asking you to do anything. I am ordering you to obey my instructions. Now, let's get on with it."

As reluctant as I was I knew that he would leave me to my death if our positions were reversed. The case he had presented was unarguable and I started to make preparations to slink out of there with my tail between my legs while David Hawk, my mentor for more years than I could recall, was left to die in my place.

"Just promise me one thing, sir," I said. "When you run out of breath, breathe through the damp towel."

"Whatever you say, Carter. But may I remind you that it is the condemned man who is supposed to be given the last request."

I dunked the towel in the pail of water, wrung it out and handed it to Hawk, then unzippered my fly and took Pierre out and went over to the door and hammered on it. I stood there with Pierre in my hand waiting for the guards to arrive. I really don't know how long it was, but it seemed like hours and still they didn't come.

I walked over to Hawk and offered him my hand. "I'm sorry it had to end this way, sir. I don't think I have to tell you how much you have meant to me."

Hawk shook my hand. "You were a good boy, Carter. One of the best I've ever had, but that doesn't excuse you from obeying my orders. Go bang on that door again."

I hammered on the rough wood with my clenched fist and willed somebody to hear me. Finally I heard the bar on the other side being released. The door opened a crack and a voice said, "What the hell is it now?"

"Mr. Hawk is ill. It's probably brain damage that he suffered when you louts beat him up."

"Stand well back, I'm coming in."

I retreated to the center of the room and stood there watching while one of the guards came in cocking his Ingram. He was followed by another and they took up positions on either side of the door. Then came the third man who seemed to be in charge of all the prisoners. Hawk had the damp towel in his hands and buried his face in it. The guy walked over and squatted beside him.

I took a deep breath, pushed the plunger of Pierre, dropped it on the floor and closed the door. Trying not to hurry so as to conserve my breath, I walked over to where Hawk sat crouched down and pushed the guard away from him. I picked Hawk up bodily and carried him out of the door.

As luck had it the guards had come from the room directly across the passage and the door was open. I took Hawk in there and lay him on the cot and went back, stopping to take another breath at the door before I went in to disarm the guards. I came out and put the bar back in place again and went back to see if I could do anything for David Hawk.

Pierre contained potassium cyanide in a gaseous form which causes a very painful and rapid death. One whiff of it will kill a man on contact. The three guards were already dead and I was hoping that I had not handled Hawk so roughly that he was forced to expel his breath and get a taste of it. I rolled him over on to his face and started pumping his rib cage. I got a wheezing sound but I had no idea of whether it was potassium cyanide or air that I was pumping out of his lungs. Then the noise of the wheezing changed its rate and I realized that Hawk was chuckling.

I straightened up and left him to roll over and sit up. "If I ever replace you with a woman operative, Carter," he said, "it will be because they are better at mouth-to-mouth resuscitation."

I helped him to his feet, stuck one of the automatics in my belt, cocked both Ingrams and adjusted their rate of fire to single shot. Then with Hawk following me I edged to the door and looked around. As far as I could see we were alone. The passage stretched both ways and all I could see were closed doors which probably meant that it was night. My watch indicated a few minutes after three but it is a twelve-hour watch and I had no way to tell whether it was day or night until I could see the sky. In any event there were no people around which was the main thing.

I led the way along the passage with Hawk at my heels until we got to the room that I had likened to a banquet room where we had been interviewed. There was still nobody in sight although I had half expected to see a guard at every crucial point. The fact that the room was empty reflected on the gross incompetence of the Children of the Revolution. All the torches had been extinguished which supported my theory that it was night. There was a very small doorway at the far end where the bearded man had been sitting and we walked over to it.

Beyond the doorway the attempts at cleaning up had only been cursory. There were great heaps of rocks and dust lay everywhere. At the far end of this room was a pair of crudely shaped double doors. If this was an Inca point of civilization as I suspected, beyond those doors lay the outside world. I'm not sure of my Inca history, but I know that they had not progressed to the point where they made wooden doors to seal off their buildings. Hawk grabbed mv arm and pointed off to our right. Close to the wall was an immense block of stone which could have served as an altar for whoever had occupied the place after the Incas. I know that the Incas were sun-worshippers and their successors had probably used it to make animal or human sacrifices. But all that was strictly conjecture and I turned my attention back to the double doors that stood between us and freedom. They hung from rough-fashioned hinges and appeared to have no fastening device. if one takes a couple of prisoners and installs them somewhere where there is no lock on the door, one must have a damned good reason for it, like an armed guard standing outside. I snicked the safety catch of the Ingram off and moved toward the doors when an ear-splitting noise assailed my ears.

It was a high-pitched wailing noise and sounded as

though it came from a hand-cranked siren; obviously a warning that we had escaped. This made it even more imperative for us to get through those doors. I started for them, meaning to break them open with a lunge of my shoulder, but Hawk grabbed my arm. As he did so, I heard the sound of running footsteps coming from behind us and at the same time there was a hammering on the outside of the doors.

Remembering how long it had taken them to open my door when I was knocking, I thought the hell with it and allowed Hawk to lead me over to the altar where we ducked down behind the shelter of the stone altar. I could hear the running footsteps getting closer and at the same time the hammering of the door became louder. Apparently those on the outside could hear the siren and were reluctant to allow their colleagues to have all the fun. They wanted to get in on the currently popular sport of chasing Americanos. Then the hammering stopped and I could hear the sound of several shoulders launched at the doors. Reminding myself how close I had come to opening those doors and rushing straight into their hands, I peered round the edge of the altar and waited to see what was going to happen.

The door burst open and the footsteps reached the doorway to the temple at the same time. As the two groups saw each other they both started firing. Not until three men lay dead did they realize what had happened. Leaving one man to guard the doorway the rest of them rushed back through the banquet room and I could hear their pounding footsteps running back throught the entire structure.

The Ingram has only a five-inch barrel which ends in

a cloth-bound silencer and there are no sights so I put it aside, cocked the Colt automatic and drew a bead on the guard. I squeezed off and he crumpled to the floor. I hoped that nobody had heard the shot or if they did would attribute it to another mistake. Hawk and I got to our feet and ran across the dead guard where I relieved him of his Ingram and the automatic while Hawk went to the other three and took the magazines out of their Ingrams. Then like a couple of truant schoolboys we walked out of the doors into the chill dawn of the mountains.

The sky was dark now except for the patch of light that heralded the dawn and all the stars were out in all their glory. But far better than the sight of the clear sky was the smell of the fresh air. After being cooped up for so long in that ancient edifice I rewarded myself with several deep breaths and I'm quite sure that Hawk did the same thing. We then started to look around, trying to figure out where we were. The building we had just left had been built on a small mountain, either so that it could serve as a fortress or so that passersby would have to look up at it. In any event it had certainly not been built for ease of access.

We found ourselves on a small, flat, rock-strewn plateau facing east. Beyond the flat there were a few straggling bushes but no sign of any trees or livestock. We had absolutely no idea of where we were except that we were in Peru. If the talks were to be conducted on an aircraft carrier, unless somebody had invented a method by which aircraft carriers could be made to climb mountains, they must be held somewhere in the Pacific Ocean, and as I had told Hawk earlier it would be downhill all the way. Peru is a large country measured from north to south and only about eight hundred miles wide; even so, eight hundred miles is one hell of a long way when you have to walk it.

The first thing that we had to do was to explore the immediate terrain. I could see from the light in the sky that we were facing east and the way to civilization lay in the opposite direction. We started to walk around the structure to see what transport we could steal, because it was obvious that Hawk and I had been transported by some means and if it could be driven up the mountain it could be driven down again. Apparently the whole place had been abandoned except for the one entrance we had used. I was starting to feel an urgency about getting out of there. There was a very definite limit to the time they would take exploring the inside, and when they found the dead guard by the door, there would be a full scale pursuit of us and I wanted to be as far as possible when the chase started.

The building, or to be more precise the ruins, had been built on a leveled mountain and judging by the chill in the air it was somewhere in the Sierra Ranges that separate the Andes from the coastal region where so much of the country's agriculture takes place. If we could get transport to head us due west it would only be a matter of time until we found a river that would lead us to the Pacific Ocean and maybe a boat with a radio. However, that appeared to be wishful thinking. By the time we had skirted the building, we found that the west side had been built flush with a sheer drop of several hundred feet. From the layout we must have been brought in by helicopter: there just wasn't any other way to get in there. As reluctant as I was to attempt the journey on foot, I started to search for a path that would lead us down the mountainside.

I had forgotten all about Hawk until he called me and then I realized that he had gone off on a foraging expedition of his own. When he called I scrambled back up the slope to where he could see me. "I've found our transport."

"I hope it's four-wheel drive, sir. We're going to need it to get down out of here."

"Well," he said. "Would you settle for four-footed drive?"

I went over to join him and just below where he stood there was a small leveled space that housed about twenty mules. We began to slide down the slope to the corral when I heard voices above us, "Come back, or we'll shoot you down."

Having got that far we weren't about to go back and it was highly unlikely that they would shoot us and defeat their own purpose. We slid down to the corral, opened the gate and picked up a couple of bridles that hung very conveniently on a post. Hawk mounted and took the bridle of the second mule and I switched the Ingram over to full automatic fire and swept the ridge where our pursuers had convened. It only had part of the effect that I had hoped for. The line of heads disappeared but the damned silencer was far too effective to stampede the mules. I dropped the Ingram with its empty magazine and drew the Colt. Three shots fired into the air and all the mules were hightailing it down a path that had been concealed by a clump of bushes, and Hawk was trying desperately to hang on to both mules.

I ran across the corral and vaulted onto the back of the mule, and like a couple of fugitives from a B-grade western, we cantered down the path in the wake of the stampeding mules.

TWELVE

It had been quite a while since I had been astride a horse and even then it had been on a comfortable saddle. If I exposed myself to very much of this I would be black and blue on the insides of my thighs. I know that Hawk played racquetball for relaxation and, if anything, his thighs would be even more susceptible to the pounding they were getting than mine. After a while the mules slowed to a dignified walk. I felt a long way short of dignified, but at least they were surefooted and I had every confidence that they would not try to shy us off over some precipice.

There was no chance of being followed until the Children of the Revolution were able to catch some of the mules and unless they looked upon the corral as home, they were likely to stray anywhere at all making pursuit even more difficult. I had no idea where the peace talks were to be held, and we had to be there in time to stop the assassination attempt on President Hernando Martinez. I had an inborn sense of urgency about the whole thing, but the best way to ride a mule is to let it take its own sweet time. It had a full belly and gave no indication of wanting to wander off the path and start grazing.

We plodded on under the lightening sky wondering just how long it would take us to cover the distance to the coast. As I remembered it the maximum distance from the coast to the mountains was about forty miles. We were riding through dense brush and I saw no sign of mountains ahead so I could not calculate the distance. The only ones in our party who seemed to know exactly where we were and where we were headed were the two mules and I deemed it best to hand over the leadership of the party to their wiser heads. Hawk was riding ahead of me and after about an hour, when I figured that we had covered about four miles, he reined in holding up his hand in the universal signal to stop.

Directly in front of him were two pieces of modern transportation left over from World War II. One was a jeep with the markings of the U.S. army; the other was a light Bedford truck similar to those used by the British army. We dismounted and tethered the mules to the first of a stand of eucalyptus trees. We did this not because we wanted to make it easier for the Children of the Revolution to find them, but because when I run across a couple of trucks just when I am needing them most I tend to get suspicious.

My suspicions were well founded in the case of the jeep. Somebody had removed the rotor arm from the distributor, but when I checked the Bedford they had only immobilized it by removing the ignition key and the high-tension lead from the leads in the jeep and hot-wired it and got the engine started while Hawk set the mules free. Ten minutes later we were rolling along a dusty, gravel road at a steady twenty miles an hour looking for the coast.

Hawk had already expressed his doubts as to where the peace talks would be held, but taking into consideration the nations involved—Peru, Ecuador, Colombia and Panama—I expected them to anchor the *U.S. Abraham Lincoln* off the coast of Ecuador or Colombia. There is a vast difference in the time taken in traveling in an ancient army truck as compared with a splay-footed mule. The mules had done a good job for us, but they could not compare with the truck. Within an hour we found ourselves pulling into the wharf of a tiny fishing village. We climbed out of the truck and left it where it was and looked over the available boats.

It was still very early in the day and like most fishermen they had gone to sea at first light. There were only half a dozen dinghies tied up at the wharf and one elderly sailing vessel of the type that is used in these waters to catch haddock, mackerel and cod. We could wait until afternoon when the fleet returned or we could try to find the owner of the one remaining boat. The entire village was a small collection of primitive huts, a cantina, a church and what appeared to be a general store.

Like most small villages their world was built around their fishing fleet. Everybody had left before dawn and there was no point in delaying the opening of the store to what we in the cities would think of as a reasonable hour. It was five-thirty by my watch and when I got to the store there were quite a number of housewives doing their weekly marketing. Behind the counter were an older couple who, from their size, looked as though they had spent most of their life sampling their wares.

All heads were turned as we entered and I addressed myself to the man. "I wish to rent a boat."

"*Si, señor*. We have a great many boats in the village but they are all out fishing. They will be back at sundown."

"There is one boat out there. Where does the captain live?"

It might have been piling it on too thick to refer to a village fisherman as captain, but a little flattery often reaps dividends. "Oh, *si, señor*. Captain Diaz is sick and unable to sail with the fleet today."

"Can you tell me where Captain Diaz lives?"

"I can do much better than that, *señor*. I can introduce you to *Señora* Diaz herself."

As he spoke, a plump woman in her early fifties holding a shopping bag came forward. With all the dignity that the storekeeper could muster, he introduced us to *Señora* Diaz. I carried her shopping bag and Hawk and I followed her out of the store to a clean but weather-beaten hut where some half-dozen kids were playing. She took us inside and introduced us to her husband, making sure that she emphasized the "captain."

He was lying on a bed covered with a couple of threadbare blankets and one look at him made me wonder how he had lasted as long as he had. His skeletal frame was wracked by harsh, constant coughing spells and from time to time he spat into a bowl and we could see the blood in the phlegm. My first thought was to find out what he had been doing to contract tuberculosis in what is normally a very healthful vocation like fishing, but that had to take its priority. The important thing was to borrow his boat.

"Captain Diaz," I started, as I perched myself on the side of his bed. I used the Peruvian accent to give him more confidence in me. Hawk speaks Spanish, but he doesn't have the ear for accents that I have. He was content to stand back and let me do the talking. "Captain Diaz, I would like to rent your boat."

"Here, a man's boat is his whole life. Why should I rent it to a stranger?"

"Because I am going to pay you very well, and you know that you will never fish again until you get new sails." I had noticed their appearance when I spotted the boat at the wharf.

"I have good sons who can fish."

"They cannot fish with those sails, and how long will it take them to earn one hundred and fifty thousand *sols* to buy the sails to replace the ones that are about to fall apart?" I had no idea what new sails would cost, but one hundred and fifty thousand *sols* was more than five hundred dollars and I tried to make it an attractive offer.

"I could not let my ship go to sea without one of my sons aboard."

I pointed to a ten-year-old boy who was helping his mother prepare vegetables for their midday meal. I knew that in a family such as this all the sons had learned to sail, probably before they had learned to walk, and he would know the coast well.

"I'll take him with me. He will be able to return the boat after my friend and I get on the big boat."

I could see he was tempted. "You would pay me a hundred and fifty thousand *sols* for this."

"No," I said. "I will pay you one hundred fifty thousand *sols* to rent the boat. I will also pay you one hundred fifty thousand *sols* to employ you son as our captain. And another one hundred fifty thousand *sols* for him to bring your boat back to you."

He looked at me suspiciously. "You have that much money?"

I started to pull my wallet out and suddenly remembered that neither of us had any Peruvian *sols,* I had a few American dollars, a few Uruguayan *pesos,* several hundred Mexican *pesos* and a couple of credit cards, and I doubted that a sick old fisherman on the coast of Peru would take Diners Club. Fortunately Hawk came to the rescue with a roll of American currency. He recognized the greenbacks and I counted them into his hand giving him the benefit of the current exchange.

He leaned back into his pillow, his pride satisfied, clutching the money.

"You drive a hard bargain, Captain Diaz," I said loud enough for his wife to hear.

He leaned forward again and spoke in a low tone so that his wife would not hear. "You are very generous, *señor*. You knew as soon as you saw me that I was dying. You could have bought the boat for a hundred thousand sols, and you knew that."

"If I had bought the boat your sons would have been deprived of their livelihood," I told him. 'This way there will be some meat on the table and some candles lit in the church for you, and your sons will still be going fishing. And believe me it was well worth it to me and my friend."

He called his son over and gave him rapid instructions to go with me wherever I wanted to go and then bring the boat back again with a warning that he would flay his hide if the boat was not tied up properly when he inspected it the next morning. Hawk and the boy walked down to the boat, but I stopped in the doorway and threw him a salute that any admiral would have been proud of. "*Vaya con Dios,* Captain Diaz."

I left him hawking into his bowl and followed the others down to the ramshackle boat where the three of us were able to raise the tattered sails and started to tack to the north. Like most fishing vessels in this part of the world its length was just enough to carry the three masts and it had the usual broad beam found on offshore fishing boats all over the world, so its pitch was very slight but we had to stand with our legs well braced to overcome the yaw. I had not been able to find out our starting point except that it was a village called Sainte Martine and any chart of the waters may have existed, but not on our boat. And as for a radio, the boy had certainly heard of a radio and went to considerable trouble to tell us about the time he had listened to the priest's radio. If it had not been for the Ingrams which we had left in the truck we might have been back in the days of the Incas.

About a mile offshore the wind shifted to almost due south and we settled down to a comfortable run before the wind until we could attract the attention of somebody with a radio. But our luck didn't last that long. As soon as I was starting to feel complacent the wind picked up and after two minutes when my hopes really soared, there was a terrible ripping sound and three quarters of the main sail fell to the deck. While the three of us began to clear the deck around our feet, the other two sails proved that they were not up to the job of propelling the boat alone and we were left with three bare masts.

This whole assignment was turning out to be a masterpiece of paradoxes: I had gone from riding in a chauffeured Rolls Royce to a barebacked mule to an ancient army truck to being stranded on a boat with no sails. Any moment I expected to be called upon to start bailing, and from there it was only a matter of time to swim around the Pacific Ocean looking for the *Abraham Lincoln*. I could tell from the looks that Hawk was sending me that he regretted leaving the guns in the truck when he felt that they may have been just reward for the situation I had got him into. But, what the hell, I didn't get him kidnapped. The boy was an entirely different proposition. I had learned that his name was Raoul and that his father had charged him with the responsibility of the family boat. When the third sail came down to lie in a tattered heap on the deck he burst into tears.

We were a long way from the rest of the fishing fleet by this time and there was nothing we could do except drift with the tide, although I was tempted to burst into tears myself. I am used to being in charge of every situation in which I find myself. When I am dealing with people I have no trouble at all, but it is a different matter when one is battling the elements. Of course there was only myself to blame. I should never have set sail without replacing the sails, but I was catering to the urgency I felt. Besides, where the hell was I going to get a new set of sails at a moment's notice.

Raoul, reluctant to give up his temporary position of captain, was standing in the bow waiting for a miracle while Hawk and I were sitting midships sharing my last two cigarettes. Whether it was Raoul's tears or prayers that did it I shall never know, but suddenly he cried out, "*Señor,* we are saved."

THIRTEEN

That may have been an exaggeration but there was certainly a small craft on its way toward us. It was a low-lying craft and we could not yet see any of the details other than it had no sails and was making far greater speed than any sailing vessel. As it got closer we could see the Peruvian national flag. It was probably a Coast Guard cutter either coming to see if we needed help, to tell us that we had drifted beyond the national limitations or to check up on our catch and to make us throw the small ones back. There was a sailor at the helm and another standing in the bow with a bullhorn. He called out, "You. Fishing vessel. Heave to."

"Heave to, indeed" I muttered. "Where the hell did he think we were going? As they moved up to us the one in the bow threw us a line and Raoul made it fast to one of the forward deck cleats. The one in the stern dropped a sea anchor over the side and they both came aboard. I was immediately disappointed with the Peruvian Coast Guard. In the States, any vessel that was boarded, was by an officer. Neither of these two had any badges of rank, one of them had a day's stubble on his chin and the other's cap was at least two sizes too small and crammed down on his head.

"Let us see your identification."

Both Hawk and I fished our wallets out and opened them to our AXE ID cards. "I need to use your radio urgently," said Hawk.

"All in good time."

"The time is right now." I could see that he was getting impatient. "Where is your officer?"

The second man who hadn't spoken yet said, "Our officer is downstairs using the radio to tell everybody that we have caught a couple of foreigners."

As he spoke they both pulled out Colt automatics and motioned us to climb aboard the cutter. Suddenly it dawned on me that rather than being saved we had fallen into the hands of the Children of the Revolution. I had noticed the holstered Colts at their waists, but the Colt is the standard equipment for the American services, and most Coast Guards wear side arms. What irked me was that from their speech I should have realized that neither of them could read English and yet they knew that we were foreigners. I should have made my move then, but it's never too late until you're dead and I had no intention of winding up in that state.

We were ushered aboard the cutter and down to the cabin below decks where a man in uniform sat with his back to us hunched over the radio. Hawk and I crowded into the confined space with Raoul being pushed along behind us. When the man at the radio heard us approaching he turned to face us. It was the bearded man we had left at the Inca ruins.

"Ah, Hawk and Carter. So nice to see you again."

"I wish I could say the same," I muttered. "How the hell did you manage to get here so fast?"

"You underestimate me, Carter. While you were plodding down the mountains on a mule which you stole, I simply climbed aboard my helicopter and watched to see where you were going."

"I would have thought you would be content to leave us adrift in the boat."

"I will be, as a fitting punishment for a couple of horse thieves, particularly now that your boat is disabled, but first we must make sure that the explosion goes off without a hitch. Then we can use your bodies to prove to the world that America has assassinated *El Presidente*."

"Nobody is going to believe that."

"America has been suspected of that kind of thing many times in the past. Surely you know that your CIA has been accused of starting the war between Iran and Iraq. Once you and Hawk have been found dead close to the assassination of President Martinez, the entire world will be on our side. There will be so much outside pressure from the rest of the world that Panama will be forced to enter a union of the countries, while I myself will take up the duties of vice president of Peru under my collaborator Tina Rodriguez."

I said, "I still don't see how you got here so fast."

"You assumed that the mules were the only transport at my headquarters. Had you walked around the building the other way you would have found my two helicopters. Need I remind you that there is a good deal of wealth behind this movement."

Hawk said, "I think it is insulting for you to kill us when we don't even know your name."

For all I cared he might have been Smokey the Bear, but Hawk was trying to keep his attention while we looked over the situation. We had left all the guns that we had taken from them in the truck. I hated to lug around a strange weapon. I am only comfortable with Wilhelmina and anything else is an encumbrance once I have passed immediate point of use.

The bearded man leaned back, lit a cigar and said, "How rude of me. I am Jaime Vasquez, you are David Hawk and Nicholas Carter, sometimes known as Nicholas Cramer. The boy I don't know."

As long as he was acting dignified, I said, "This is Captain Raoul Diaz." The tears had long since stopped and the boy stood up to his full height and his face glowed with pride.

Still trying to keep his attention, Hawk said, "Where did you get the boat from? I can understand how you might have bought a helicopter, but the Coast Guard doesn't sell its cutters."

"I have bought not one but two helicopters and I have two very competent pilots to fly them for me. The Ingram M10 submachine gun is a very persuasive argument when one is looking for a boat. As a matter of fact it even persuaded the crew to lend us their uniforms. When my helmsman spotted you I was trying to tune in to the *Abraham Lincoln*'s radio frequency to find out where they were."

"But if you have already set the explosive why

would you want to do that?"

"I haven't done it myself. Some of my colleagues have been aboard since it sailed and I must leave you and Carter at the scene for the utmost effect."

I said, "Your fight is with me and Hawk. You don't need the boy. Put him back on board his boat and set him loose for somebody to find him."

"On the contrary, I do need him. I had intended to kill you and set your boat afire, but it will be far more effective this way. Losing your sails will only emphasize your incompetence. Too bad about the boy, but that's the way it goes sometimes." To his "sailors" he said, "Take them up on deck and tie them up."

He turned back to the radio while his men hustled us up to the deck. Then covering Hawk and myself with the Colts, they made Raoul tie our hands and feet. When he finished they tied him up and went back to their posts, towing the Diaz boat behind as they sailed north again.

We were left lying in a heap with Raoul between us. He looked up at me with his tear-stained face and said, "Does this mean that they're going to kill us, *señor*?"

"I'm afraid so, Raoul."

"*Madre de Dios,*" he said, "my father will kill me if anything happens to his boat."

I said, "Jaime Vasquez is going to save him the trouble." I was working on the knots that bound my wrists, but Raoul had done too good a job on them and there was very little likelihood of loosening them. Then I thought of the obvious.

"You've tied these knots well, Raoul. You must be a very good sailor."

"I am, *señor*. If I tie a knot it stays tied."

"Are you a good enough sailor to always carry a knife with you?"

"*Señor,* I am never without my knife."

"Why the hell didn't you say so before?" said Hawk.

"Nobody asked me, *señor.*"

"Where is it?" I asked.

"On the back of my belt under my shirt."

"Turn your back to me." I felt him turn and I turned away from him and under the thin shirt he wore I felt the handle of the sheath knife. I pulled it out and slashed at Raoul's bonds and then felt him take the knife from my hand and a moment later my hands were free and there was a trickle of blood running down my hands.

I took the knife back from him and cut the rope that tied my feet and then set Hawk free. I returned the knife to Raoul who replaced it in its sheath. We had been left lying on the deck aft of the cabin so that the man standing in the bow was hidden from our view but I could see the man at the helm. He was standing well back, relaxed with one hand resting lightly on the wheel. He was watching the compass and from time to time making minor adjustments to his course.

I crawled forward on my belly trusting that his attention would be taken up by watching the compass and that he wouldn't notice me. I need not have worried, for the Children of the Revolution this was merely a pleasant morning's cruise. I actually got to within ten feet of him before he spotted me.

I had been watching his feet and legs and making sure that I didn't stumble over anything on deck. I saw his legs suddenly tense up and I bunched my legs under me and hurled myself at him just as he was clawing at the holstered Colt.

I swept the gun aside and clamped my right hand around his throat and squeezed. There was no room for either of us to move so I was unable to practice any of my karate moves. The only thing I could do was to hang onto his throat and try to keep my balance. I squeezed until he went red in the face and his tongue lolled out. Then his eyeballs popped and his sphincter relaxed. I picked him up bodily and tossed him overboard and looked around me.

Hawk was squatting on the deck with Raoul beside him waiting to see what I was going to do. The man in the bow had not moved. He stood by the furthermost section of the rail looking straight ahead completely unaware of what had been going on behind him. I stood behind the helm and swung it violently from left to right and back again. The sudden movement of the prow caught him off balance and he clutched at the rail in a vain attempt to save himself before he joined his buddy in the clear waters of the Pacific.

He was not the only one caught off balance. There was a crash from below decks followed by cursing in Spanish that Raoul should never have been subjected to . . . Jaime Vasquez climbed the companionway to the deck. Hawk let him get up to his level and launched himself at him. Hawk is not a very big man but he is all muscle.

He hit Vasquez with a solid shoulder right around the chest. Vasquez swung a punch at Hawk's head but he slipped it. I was too intent on keeping the boat weaving to make sure that Vasquez would not have a solid footing for his two hundred and fifty odd pounds, and I know that Hawk can give a pretty good account of himself. Vasquez landed a haymaker on Hawk's chest, and he responded with a left jab to the solar plexus just as I swung the wheel again. Vasquez, caught off balance, again and went back to finish up with his back to rail. Hawk followed him up raining lefts and rights on his chest and head. I steadied the boat and let him have at it.

Hawk had poised himself on the balls of his feet and, from the rocklike stance, he was putting more muscle into his blows than I would have thought possible. The finish came with a left jab to the solar plexus. Vasquez straightened up for a right hook. He saw it coming and ducked away from it and into one of the neatest left uppercuts I have ever seen. Vasquez's eyes glazed and he fell forward to lie in the scuppers.

I looked across at Hawk and gave him the old sign of thumb and forefinger in an "O," but it was not all over yet. As he lay there on the deck and Hawk walked away from him, Vasquez fished under his uniform jacket and brought out another Colt automatic. From where he lay on the deck he he swung the pistol around to draw a bead on Hawk.

From the other side of the deck came a bloodcurdling yell and a figure hurtled across the intervening space. There was the gleam of a highly polished knife blade and Raoul looked up from where Vasquez's wrist lay pinned to the deck and picked up the pistol. He handed it to Hawk. "Will you teach me how to use one of these, *señor?*"

"Don't you wish you'd asked him if he had a knife?" I asked Hawk.

Hawk threw his arm around the boy's shoulders. "Come, let's go find out where we are, while Nick does the steering." They climbed down the companionway to the radio like a couple of schoolboys who had just won their first basketball game.

I corrected our course to a little west of due north and went over to where Jaime Vasquez lay. Raoul was a lot stronger than I would have thought. The razor-keen edge had been thrust through the arm between the two bones, severing the artery and had penetrated a good inch into the wooden deck. I pulled the knife out and wiped it on Vasquez's uniform jacket. I picked up the body and tossed it over the side then looked around for something to wash the deck. I found a bucket with a rope attached and threw several buckets of seawater over the deck to remove the blood.

I was steering by guesswork and after about fifteen minutes Raoul came up the companionway to stand by my side and watch me. "*Señor* Hawk," he said, "told me to tell you to steer fifteen degrees west of north and we will meet the big boat in ten miles. And he is going to teach me to use the pistol."

I ruffled his hair. "I think you will be a very good pistolero." Knowing what small boys are like, I added, "Are you hungry?"

"*Si, señor*. I am always hungry."

"They will have some very good food on the big boat."

I stood there trying to answer his questions about the big boat. When I told him that it had a lot of airplanes on it I could see that he didn't believe me. If he had ever seen an airplane, which I doubted, it was from the ground as it flew overhead, and the largest boat he had ever seen was probably about forty feet long. How do you explain an aircraft carrier with jet planes to a kid like that?

After a while Hawk came up puffing on a cigar. I said, "I don't suppose you found any cigarettes down there, did you?"

"You should have searched the sailors before you tossed them overboard."

"I guess I can wait until we reach the aircraft carrier."

"I've just been talking to them."

"I figured you had."

"I have started a search of the conference room on the *Abraham Lincoln,* and the President's quarters of the *Peruvian Queen.*"

"The *Peruvian Queen?*"

"The *Peruvian Queen* is the personal yacht of the President of Peru. From what our late friend said I figured that this explosion would either take care of everybody at the conference, or would bc a personal attack on the President himself."

"Well you should have enough manpower to find it wherever it is."

"These guys are crafty and capable, but we'll find it."

"We'd better. They won't have our dead bodies to leave at the scene, but it still won't look good if there's an explosion at the conference."

"It's still a bigger job than you might think."

"You certainly must have enough manpower to search an aircraft carrier and a yacht."

"We have, but the reason we sent an aircraft carrier

was so that the heads of state could fly in. And instead of that, they all chose to make this a vacation cruise and came in their personal yachts. It must look like a broody duck with a string of ducklings out there."

"Even so, we only have to search the conference room in the aircraft carrier and the Peruvian yacht."

"Carter, don't you think we might be taking too much for granted?"

"Like what, sir?"

"You have dealt with a great many terrorists and revolutionaries in your time. Have you ever known one of them to stick to the truth out of sheer principle?"

"Do you mean that the President of Peru might not be the target?"

"We have only Vasquez's word for it that he is working with Tina Rodriguez and we have not checked her out thoroughly. She could have been bought off by some other revolutionary group in Panama, Colombia or Ecuador. Once they had assassinated the government head she could move into the country and set herself up as president."

"She wouldn't get far without Vasquez's army behind her."

"But what I'm saying is that it might not be the Peruvian yacht that will be sabotaged. Remember, Vasquez said that one of his men had been aboard since it had sailed. I asked them to do a double check on the personnel on the aircraft carrier, but it could be any one of those personal yachts."

"I don't see what good it would do for Tina Rodriguez."

"Power, Carter. The greatest incentive of all. There

are countless millionaires all over the world, and do you know what keeps them fighting? It's not for the joy of making more money, or some hidden sex perversion; it's power. Ask any head of state why he ran for office. If he's completely honest, he will tell you that it was for the power. We are able to keep a close check on our politicians in the States and keep the country fairly free of graft, but what would happen if somebody like Rodriguez gets to head up a country, even one as small as Ecuador or Panama. The first thing we know she would be sitting in the U.N. making unreasonable demands."

"Are you saying that with or without Vasquez, she may have an ambition to take over some country other than Peru?"

"My money is on Panama as an alternative to Peru. The Panama Canal has cropped up in every conversation we have had with Vasquez. Too bad we'll never get the truth out of him now. We just can't take a chance on it. We have to expect them to make some kind of double play."

"Sir, I'll stick to Peru."

"You're unreasonable, Carter."

"The Panama Canal is a great source of potential wealth, but we have to consider where the funds originated from. The Peruvian lead mines produce vast quantities of gold that financed this thing from the beginning; not to mention the stolen Nazi hoard that Vasquez discovered in Peru. Rodriguez might have her eye on the Panama Canal but only as a colony of the Peruvian Empire. Seems to me that she would revel in being called the 'Empress Christina' of the Peruvian Empire."

"Any more ideas, Carter?"

"Yes, sir. Suppose we're both right. Suppose the plan is for a mass assassination attempt on the heads of all the governments concerned. There would then be at least four countries that would be ready to be taken over by the Children of the Revolution."

FOURTEEN

At that point our conversation died off without resolution and we turned our attention to the cutter that was approaching us. I sent Raoul up to the bow to make their line fast; Raoul was very proud of his work and I wanted to give him every opportunity to show the American sailors just how good he was. Hawk transferred to the other boat promising to meet us when we reached the *Abraham Lincoln*.

I got a course correction from a lieutenant JG who came aboard and then I let Raoul sail us back to the aircraft carrier. It was a short run and when we got there, we tied up the Peruvian Coast Guard cutter and the Diaz fishing boat. I sent Raoul down to the mess where he ate three steaks and a bucketful of french fries. I got hold of the lieutenant JG and had him take Raoul on a tour of the aircraft carrier. It was the greatest day of his life and I doubted that he would ever stop talking about the airplanes landing on the deck of the "big boat."

I think he was disappointed that we didn't fit him out with sails so that he could return home by himself. Still, I'm sure he enjoyed being towed by a real U.S. Naval cutter and being allowed to steer and give the orders to tie up the family boat. When he had left I turned to Hawk who was leaning against the rail with a glint of amusement in his eye talking to Admiral Boyd, with the usual cigar in his mouth.

Hawk must have been looking forward to this trip to the *Abraham Lincoln* because he had sent ahead for a box of his favorite cigars. The one he had filched from Vasquez's supply was a good Havana, and in both appearance and aroma was way ahead of his usual source of nicotine. He stopped talking to Admiral Boyd and turned his attention to me.

"You'd better go down to the conference room, Nick," he said. "The admiral's security force can find no trace of any explosive down there. I have assured them that with your luck you can find it easily."

I ignored Hawk's comment. If he thought it was luck that brought these assignments to a successful conclusion instead of my hard work, let him think so. After all he was my boss.

I found a lieutenant, a petty officer and a bunch of SPs in the conference room. I explained to the lieutenant what I wanted. He told me that he had received the same instructions radioed from the Naval cutter as Hawk came to the aircraft carrier. At that time they had literally taken the room apart and put it back together again.

I felt sorry for them, but I had no other choice than to order them to go through it all again. I made them take all the pictures off the walls and examine them. They turned every chair and couch upside down and inspected the stiching on the underside. They went over the walls with magnetic stethoscopes. They even had one of those flexible tubes with a light and a mirror at the end that they poked into the airconditioner ventilators. Two men lay on their backs on the carpet and examined the underside of the conference table. Metal detectors had searched every inch of the walls, floors, ceilings and furniture. I was about to give up, tell the lieutenant that he was right and tell Hawk that the assassination attempt must be made on one of the personal yachts when he appeared in the doorway.

"Where did you find it, Nick?"

"There's nothing here, sir."

The lieutenant and the SPs looked at Hawk in awe. I doubt very much that anyone had heard his name, but it was obvious that when he spoke everything on the ship came to a stop until he was satisfied. There were temporary "no smoking" signs that all the sailors were expected to conform to, and in deference to them I had not been smoking, but Hawk came in with an inch of ash on his foul-smelling weed. "It's here, all right, Nick. All you have to do is find it."

It's not often that I become defensive, and I suppose it was in defense of the sailors that I said, "This room is clean, sir."

"Carter, there is explosive hidden in this room. Now find it." As he spoke he turned away from me and as he did the ash fell from his cigar. He brushed at the remnants on his vest and ground the ash into the carpet at his feet.

Suddenly, I saw something and pounced on the carpet at his feet. I came up with a sliver of wood about half an inch long and about an eighth of an inch wide. "Now we know where it is," I said. "Give me a hand, lieutenant." Actually it took four of us to tilt the enormous table sideways, and four more to lay it on its side.

"What are we looking for now?" asked the lieutenant.

"This is a wood shaving, so they must have bored holes in the bottom of the legs of the conference table to hide the explosive. I took a knife from one of the sailors and pried up the metal cap on the bottom of the leg. Somebody had bored a hole a half inch in diameter and filled it with plastique. At the base of the cavity there was a tiny capsule. I gave that to the lieutenant and told him to take it to the gunnery officer for a report.

It was only a few seconds work to remove the explosives from the other three legs. We found a capsule-shaped fuse with every wad of explosive. There are several methods of detonating explosives; shock, heat and electric current are the most popular, but the most infallible is shock, and any charge of explosive will detonate in sympathy if a similar charge is exploded near it. Whoever had planted the plastique there had not been taking any chances. If for any reason one of them didn't explode in sympathy it had its own fuse, making sure that the whole thing would explode.

When we had cleared the plastique out of the conference table legs I was in a much better frame of mind and even Hawk was smiling benignly, a complete change from his usual scowl. The lieutenant who had been in charge of the security detachment came back with a report from the gunnery officer.

"That was a fulminate of mercury fuse and would have detonated in another twenty-four hours."

I thanked him and turned back to Hawk. "What I can't understand, sir, is why they didn't detonate them today, the first day of the talks."

He dragged on his cigar again and said, "Today wasn't the first day of the talks. Yesterday was."

I said, "That makes it even more difficult to understand. Why didn't they blow it up as soon as they got all the bigwigs sitting around the table, instead of waiting another two more days?"

"They were waiting for us, Carter."

"The conference could have started without us."

"Yes, the conference could have started without us, but without us they would not have had anybody to blame the assassination attempts on. Remember, we decided that they must be waiting for our dead bodies to leave at the scene of the assassination. Apparently, after they had caught us they decided to wait a couple of days to make sure that our corpses were in the right place at the right time."

"Jaime Vasquez would have had a lot to answer for if we hadn't already taken care of him."

"Instead of worrying about him I want you to go over each of these personal yachts, looking for explosives."

"You still think that there would be a second attempt on each one of these government heads, then?"

"I guess we never finished our conversation, but I

still think that the prime target of the assassination attempts would be the President of Panama."

"Sir, I hate like hell to disagree with you, but I still think that President Martinez of Peru is the most likely victim."

"If you cannot find any explosive on the Panamanian yacht, you have my permission to follow up on your alternative theory."

"Yes, sir. May I have the security detachment to help me search?"

"You've got it, and hurry it up, will you. Now that we have disposed of the explosive in the aircraft carrier I have given them permission to go back to their conference. Give them a couple of hours talking, and we'll give them dinner on board and then they'll want to go back to their own yachts to their mistresses or whatever waits for them."

I rounded up the lieutenant, the chief petty officer and their squad of sailors and a boat and we took off for the Panamanian yacht. Hawk had called them and they were expecting us and gave us total cooperation. I am always astounded at the amount of money that is expended on the creature comforts of those "poor" nations' leaders. I have noticed the same thing with the leaders of communist cells abroad. Although the Americans are hated for their capitalistic ideas, I notice that the communistic types trying to overthrow us drive their Cadillacs and Mercedes Benzes, while many of our senators, when not using official cars, use stripped down compacts. Panama may be a poor nation, but the President's yacht didn't reflect any sign of poverty.

The Presidential quarters had plum-colored carpet, matching silk drapes and solid teak paneled walls from which an array of Monets, Cezannes and Rembrandts looked down on us peasants from their spotlighted areas. It was not likely that anybody would buy originals for a yacht which might be sunk momentarily, but they were damned good copies.

The first mate stood there watching while we searched the place. First the pictures were lifted down and inspected on both sides, the carpet where it wasn't fastened down was rolled up, all the couch cushions were thoroughly inspected, then the couch and all the chairs were turned upside down and all the stitching inspected. They were having such a good time that I didn't want to spoil their fun, but finally I said, "How about the same place?"

The lieutenant looked at me, "The same place?"

"The same place we found the explosives on the aircraft carrier."

They ordered a couple of sailors who were just looking through the medicine cabinet in the President's bathroom into the dining room and had them tilt the dining room table over on its side and pry the plastique from the hollowed out legs.

I had already obtained Hawk's permission to follow up on my own theory of President Martinez's assassination being the prime factor of these talks, and the takeover of the Panama Canal being only a secondary issue. However, there is a stubborn streak that fits me like an angelic halo and I wanted to give Hawk every benefit of the doubt before I proved that I was right.

When we finished with the Panamanian yacht we

found plastique hidden in the hollowed out legs of the dining room table on the Ecuadorian and Colombian yachts. Four out of five told me something. It told me that the Children of the Revolution were very determined and that they had very little imagination. I could see Jaime Vasquez in that light, but it didn't ring true of Tina Rodriguez.

After all it was Tina who had put the frozen curare in my drink to get me out of the picture and I expected greater things of Tina than a repetition of the same old method. When we got to the Peruvian yacht we were met by the captain who had heard of the attempts on the other yachts and on the aircraft carrier and was only too pleased to welcome us aboard, even though he didn't think it could happen on his ship.

Gossip spreads like the proverbial wildfire even between anchored ships but I guess that a good grapevine knows no limitations.

By now the search team had dropped into a routine, and the first place they looked was the legs of the dining room table. I was there to see that we had drawn a blank this time and watched them start to figuratively take the room apart. We went through his bedroom, bathroom, sitting room and dining room, pried into every air-conditioner ventilator, rolled back every carpet and checked every radio and television set for bugs, and even checked the water pipes into his bathroom.

After a long hour I had to admit that I was wrong. The assassination attempt had been made on the four government heads attending the talks and if anything went wrong they had a supplementary system by which they could assassinate the heads of Panama, Ecuador and Colombia. That didn't make sense but before I left President Martinez's yacht I leaned over the rail and smoked a cigarette to figure it out. If the idea had been to shift the blame onto Hawk and myself for the assassinations it just didn't make sense. They had tried to blow up the conference to kill off everybody attending the talks, but we hadn't bothered to look for a booby-trap aimed at the American delegates simply because Hawk and I should have been there to take the blame for it. But that would work only if somebody from Peru, Panama, Ecuador or Colombia was killed. I was certain that the main target was President Martinez of Peru. I had not even considered Hawk's alternate theory, and now I had every opportunity to find an assassination attempt on Martinez's life, and I couldn't damn well find it.

I flipped my cigarette butt into the water and started to head for the companionway for a last look around before calling Hawk and eating crow. Like everybody else, I hate like hell to call my boss to tell him that my idea was a miserable failure. Down in the President's quarters I looked around. All the carpeting, the drapes and all the pictures on the wall and all the upholstery had been thoroughly inspected. I was still convinced that I was right and that the attempt was to have been made on President Martinez. I walked up to the captain and said, "Can you tell me who has been in President Martinez's quarters in the last two days."

"No one, *señor,*" he said. "Just our usual staff."

"Can you tell me who the usual staff are?"

"When we are at sea, no outsiders have access, naturally, but I will send a man down with a list of all the people. It will be a very short list; the valet, the steward, who makes the bed and puts out fresh towels and tidies up. Beyond that, *señor,* nobody would have any cause to go into the President's quarters."

I wandered into the bedroom and bathroom looking around. I lifted the top of the cistern to make sure that it hadn't been booby-trapped. About the time that a hand grenade was invented somebody also thought of the idea of wiring the pin to the arm of the toilet, which was probably one of the earliest booby traps, but the Children of the Revolution were not known for their originality.

Out in the bedroom there was a king-sized bed with a royal blue velvet bedspread to match the carpet and the draperies. On either side of the bed was a nightstand with a lamp on it. One of them had a few books on it. I read somewhere that you can tell a lot about a man from the books he reads, and I have never found that to let me down yet. I glanced over the titles. I was flipping through the books just in case somebody had inserted something between two of the pages, when the valet came in and handed me a list. There were three names on it.

"Who are they?" I asked.

"The top name is me, *señor*. I have been with *El Presidente* for ten years, and I always travel with him. The second name is the steward who takes the housekeeper's place when we are on the yacht and the third name is the electrician."

Why did the electrician come in here?"

"This morning *El Presidente* complained that one of the lightbulbs was out. The electrician replaced it."

"I looked up at the chandelier and flipped the switch, all the bulbs lighted up while the valet tried the ones in the bathroom. Then without touching anything I leaned over the nightstand that had the books on it, then I told the valet to tell the lieutenant to come down immediately.

When he arrived he was curious to see what I had turned up that his men had missed. "Are all your men still here, lieutenant?" I asked.

"Yes, sir, we're waiting for you."

I gave him the list of names. "The bottom one is the electrician. I want him placed under arrest, taken ashore and turned over to the Peruvian police."

"What have you found, Mr. Carter?"

"Do it. You can ask why later."

His face flushed and he hurried up on deck. If it had been me who had built the booby-trap I would have been long gone, even if I had to swim all the way to Lima, and I suspected that it would take them a while to find him. I heard the steady tramp of feet on the deck as the orders were given out. It was half an hour before the lieutenant came back. "We found him hiding in one of the stockrooms. He's in handcuffs. Now, will you tell me what you found?"

I said, "The President found a light globe wasn't working in the chandelier. Probably our friend here had loosened it so that he would be called down here. When he came down here all he had to do was to tighten the globe that he had loosened and then switch globes in his reading lamp."

I knelt on the the floor and pulled out the cord of the light that was on the nightstand, then carefully unscrewed the bulb and handed it to the lieutenant. He looked at it, shook it and said, "It looks as though it's burned out."

I took it from his hand and said, "It looks burned out, and it rattles when you shake it. But let me tell you something, lieutenant, this bulb is a long way from being burned out. It looks black because it has been filled with black powder and what you hear is not the burned-out filaments but the black powder being shaken inside the globe. Somebody took a file and cut a hole in the globe and filled it with black powder, the same stuff the muzzle-loaders use. That's why this small patch of adhesive tape is there, to seal the hole. Can you imagine what would happen if the President turned on his reading lamp. Nobody leans back when they turn on a reading lamp. It would splatter his head all over the suite. Now I'm going to have the enormous pleasure of telling my boss that I was right."

FIFTEEN

When I got back to the *Abraham Lincoln* I found Hawk sitting in the mess steadily chomping on a steak. I ordered one of the same and for a while the only sound in that corner of the mess was the steady workmanlike sound of teeth in operation. Hawk finished first and pushed his plate away from him and lit a cigar. Well, I should have known better than to sit at the same table with him. When I finished I called for more coffee and lit a cigarette. I missed my own brand, but I had been able to buy a reasonable substitute at the mess.

We sat there smoking and drinking coffee in complete silence. Around us several officers came in and started their evening meal. The silence continued. I was afraid that anything I said would sound like, ''I told you so'' and I think that Hawk was afraid of saying something that might sound like praise. We sat in what I have heard described as being akin to the silence brought about by a marital spat.

Finally, Hawk flicked the ash off his cigar and pushed his chair back. "Carter," he said, "when I was just a young shaver trying to get into this business I had a boss who I respected very much and from whom I learned a great deal, but the most important thing I learned from him came at a time when I had just completed a very difficult mission. I put in a report and I knew that I had done an excellent job and I expected to be complimented by my boss. He read my report, then he put his spectacles away and said to me, 'Young Hawk, one day you will be running this department, so when that day comes if you follow this advice you will never make a mistake.' I was just a punk kid, but I wanted to make an impression. 'What is the advice?' I asked. He said, 'Never hire a man who isn't smarter than you.' In all the years I have been running AXE I have never forgotten that advice."

I stubbed out my cigarette and lit another. "Your point is well taken, sir," I conceded.

"Don't forget you owe me a report. I'd like it tomorrow morning before they take you ashore."

"I'll write it up tonight, sir."

"I realize that it will be only a partial report. It will have to go in the file to wait for my report and the one from Butch Ramirez, but there is still a lot of work to do. Once you have reported to the Treasury people they will owe us a favor, and I am not averse to collecting from those kind of people."

"Sir, I'll work out all the details with Winters on the raids on the foundry. They should get a good haul of people to fill up their Mexican jails. There might be some legal question as to who owns the gold. I guess it will come under the heading of buried treasure even though it was only buried for forty years, so Peru has first claim on it even though it is located in Mexico. I don't know how much claim the Germans would have on it, but it was the proceeds of war crimes, and it is probably teeth fillings, wedding bands, etc., so there would be no way to trace the original owners, but we'll have to let the lawyers worry about that. The lawyers can sort out the claims. We know what happened which is all that concerns us. I'll get the American police to track down the place where they separate the gold and maybe we'll fill a few American jail cells."

"When you get it all finished I shall need a copy of your final report."

"Where will you be, sir?"

"I shall stay on here until the talks are finished, which under the circumstances shouldn't be too long. Then I have a little chore to do which will take me a couple of days. After that I shall be back in my office."

"Would that little chore involve a trip to Sainte Martine by any chance?"

"Carter, you heard me promise the boy that I would teach him how to shoot a handgun."

"I'm very glad you decided to do that, sir. If you hadn't, I was planning on something similar."

"You know what they say about great minds thinking alike. I also thought I might try to drum up some kind of a medal. I wonder if Admiral Boyd's uniform would fit me."

"If not, sir, I'm sure Admiral Boyd would be happy to accompany you."

I stood up stubbing out my cigarette. "Sir, I have to

go write a report.'' I pushed my chair back and as I left I dropped my hand on his shoulder. ''Sir, I'm very happy that you chose to go to Sainte Martine.''

He let me get all the way to the door of the mess before he called me back. I came back and stood looking down at him. ''Sir?''

''Carter, did I ever tell you that I'm glad you can hold your breath for three minutes.''

I couldn't think of an appropriate answer to that so I just said, ''Good night, sir,'' and walked out of the mess to the cabin they had found for me.

I got some writing paper and laboriously wrote out the report that Hawk expected from me. There are parts of my job as an AXE operative I like, witness my riding around in chauffeured Rolls Royces, and there are parts that I dislike, like riding bareback on a splay-footed mule, but nothing gives me so much trouble as writing a report. When the times comes I know what to do, but sometimes explaining my actions in writing takes more out of me than a good workout with five black belts, which is why I always prefer to give my reports orally. This time I could see the necessity for it because Hawk's personal report and that of Butch Ramirez would need to be coordinated with mine. I gave thanks that I had been able to bring Hawk back with me, or I would have had to spend the rest of my life writing reports.

I finally got through it, then took a shower and slipped in between the cool sheets for a good night's sleep. The next morning I used a borrowed toothbrush and a borrowed razor and joined Hawk at breakfast. I handed him the written report. He glanced at it and stuffed it into his pocket and said, "I was just talking to the President. He's very glad I'm back."

"So am I, sir," I said. "I don't think I could have faced up to all those written reports if I had left you in the ruins back there." After breakfast I went down to the radio room and had them cut in on the phone lines and connect me with Paul Winters in Tijuana. He was pretty teed off with me.

"When you work for the Treasury Department you are expected to make frequent reports. One doesn't just wander off into the blue and then call in once a month to let your supervisor know where to send your paychecks."

It had never occurred to me that they were going to pay me. I have a salary and an unlimited expense account from AXE which is quite sufficient for my needs. I said, "You needn't bother paying me."

"So that's how it is, is it? The job is too much for you."

"I've found the gold and I'm resigning from the Treasury Department."

"I hope that doesn't mean that we can have what's left after you get through with it."

"You wouldn't say that to my face, Winters. I shall be in Quito, Ecuador, in half an hour. I shall catch the next plane to Mexico City. I want you to meet me at the airport."

"What time will you be there? I don't have any idea of the flight schedules from here. I shall probably have to go to San Diego."

"If there is one thing that South America is famous

for it's a lack of sense of timing. We'll meet sometime in the next couple of days."

"Why Mexico City?"

"Because that's where the gold is."

"Then why are you going to Quito?"

"It's a long story, Winters, which doesn't concern you or the Treasury Department. Sufficient to say that I have found the source of the black market gold so there will be no more smuggling. It will be mere routine to pick up the American side of the organization."

"I hope you know what you're doing, Carter."

There have been countless times when I could have said that myself, but I cut him off and went up to the flight deck.

We must have drifted considerably further north than I had anticipated because once in the helicopter we headed almost due east for Quito. Apparently they had arranged the meeting place as far north as possible to make it a central location for Panama, Ecuador, Colombia and Peru. Once we set down at the international airport at Quito I once more became a slave to the South American policy of "Manana," but by flashing my ID in the airport manager's office, and again in the airline's office I was able to determine that there really was a plane leaving that day for Mexico City.

Finding out that it was scheduled to leave that day was a long way from the actual fact, and it was three hours late taking off. It was the middle of the night before we touched down at Mexico City. Winters was waiting for me. Of course he had every advantage over me; he was flying an American airline which departed from an American city. He appeared to be pleased to see me which may have been because I refused to take him into my confidence about all the complicated ramifications of the case, but also may have been due to the fact that he felt sympathetic toward anybody who had been sentenced to fly from any South American city. Whatever it was I was grateful for it. It was about time for me to bow out of the scene leaving Winters in sole charge of the case and acting as liaison officer between the American Treasury and Customs and the Mexican authorities.

He had a Mexican police inspector with him, and with Winters driving and me guiding him we went out to the foundry. It was the early hours of the morning and not yet light. The inspector was all in favor of bursting in and seizing the gold, but Winters put his foot down and made him wait until the factory had started work so that they could get everybody involved.

I went back to police headquarters with them and helped to plan the raid. I told them that they would find a considerable amount of gold and Winters called his superior at the Treasury Department who would start a search for the separation unit. We decided to wait until nine o'clock in the morning before going in and seizing the gold so that we could catch the maximum number of people. Both Winters and myself cautioned everybody involved in the raid that it was to be carried out in the utmost secrecy. The police were only too happy to cooperate on this matter.

The Mexican police may have put too much faith in the old adage that possession is nine points of the law and may have thought that whatever we recovered would belong to the Mexican government. Personally, I expected a long, drawn-out hassle over ownership. What was worrying me about the whole thing was that if word had leaked out, Tina or McBride would have sent in a team to retrieve it, which was why I had insisted on absolute secrecy.

Rather than leave police headquarters where somebody might sneak a look at the plans for the raid, we sent out for breakfast and ate it around the inspector's desk. I had just missed another night's sleep but I had slept well the previous night, so it wouldn't bother me. When we finished breakfast we sat around smoking cigarettes and drinking coffee until it was time to move.

We used six police cars, three at the front and three at the back and a couple of vans to transport the prisoners to the jail. I followed the inspector into the front door. He stood inside the front door, blew his whistle and yelled, "Don't move. Everybody is under arrest." It was the closest thing to a raid on a speakeasy I have ever seen off the movie screen.

Cops swarmed through the place and I saw several of them speak to the workers only to be answered with a shake of the head. The cops had been told that we were going to seize contraband gold, and some of them seemed surprised when they couldn't see it.

Naturally it was hidden where it could not have been easily seen, and then I had a horrible thought. Suppose Tina had had me followed that night or had somehow managed to get to Butch Ramirez's report and moved the gold. If I had talked the Treasury Department and the Mexican police into pulling this raid and then couldn't find any gold my popularity rating would sink to the level of a bear in a beehive.

I was wondering why I hadn't left a message with Butch Ramirez to contact Winters with the full story when the inspector called me in, "Now where is all this gold you spoke of, *Señor* Carter?"

I took him over to the paint storage room. I was about to break the lock when the foundry manager appeared. "Please do not break anything. You people have done quite enough damage to my day's productivity." He produced a key and opened the padlock and swung the door open.

The inspector said, "Where is all the gold? All I see are paint cans."

"You haven't seen the insides yet," I told him. I picked up a paint drum and carried it across to the paint trough, picked up a screwdriver and opened the lid and poured the paint into the trough. The manager started to get very excited. "No, no, *señor*. We cannot pour the paint straight in. It has to be stirred first."

I ignored him and kept pouring. The paint flowed smoothly with its full gold color flecked with the transparency of the thinning liquid they used. As I reached the bottom of the can and the flow of the paint started to falter I was surprised at how light the drum had become. According to my calculations there should have been three inches of gold in the bottom, but it felt like I was holding an empty can. A fact that was emphasized by the inspector who had a very unsociable expression on his face.

I was about to ask Winters and the inspector what form of suicide they recommended when I had an idea, something that had been missing since I started this case. Some of these workers must be innocent. When you are dealing with several hundred million dollars worth of gold you try to keep it a secret, because if you don't, you are going to get ripped off. Whenever the worker who was responsible for keeping the paint trough topped up needed a new can he would take one from the top and pour it in. I led the way back into the paint room again and started pulling paint drums down until I could reach one from the bottom row, then I repeated my performance of pouring the paint out with considerably more confidence. By the time the drum was empty it was obvious to everybody that I was right and the inspector had handcuffs on the foundry manager, and a team of policemen were pouring gold paint into whatever receptacle they could find.

It was the first time in the history of the Federal Reserve Bank of Mexico that they had been asked to store a load of dirty paint cans in their vault, but we left them with the inspector promising that he would arrange for somebody to remove the gold and discard the drums and work the gold into more manageable form for their storage space.

We went back to police headquarters where the inspector began the thankless task of separating those who would be charged from those who were innocent. It was clear that the foundry manager knew what had been going on, but that the majority of the workers had been in complete ignorance.

The inspector left the room to answer some questions about the charges being made, and when he returned he took me by the arm and led me to a corner of the room.

"*Señor,*" he said in a conspiratorial whisper. "I have just discovered that the owner of the foundry is none other than *Señora* Tina Rodriguez."

I removed his hand from my arm and prodded him in the chest with a forefinger. "In America we have a set of laws, and these laws are the same for rich people as for poor people. I was hoping it was the same here."

"Oh, yes, *señor*. It is."

"In that case when you arrest Tina Rodriguez," I said, "you'd better pick up Curtis McBride, her executive vice president. He may not be guilty, but he's entitled to prove that in court."

Before I left police heaadquarters I made a phone call to Washington. I could have done it from outside but I am no stranger to the ways of the Mexican telephone systems, and I thought that calling from police headquarters would minimize the "manana" attitude. I was lucky, it only took forty-five minutes to get through. It was early evening there and when it rang three times without being answered I thought that Natalie must have gone out. Then, halfway through the fifth ring it was picked up and I heard Natalie's breathless voice. "Hello."

"It's me. Nick."

"Did you get me out of the shower just to tell me that?"

"I called to tell you that I'll be in Washington in a couple of days."

"I'm not sure you should have called. I'm mad at you."

"Now why would a nice girl like you be mad at a real sweet guy like me?"

"I waited a week for you to make a pass at me, and when you invited me over to your apartment on the Saturday night I thought that was it. I put on my best dress and my black lace underwear and when I arrived all you did was give me a drink and then puttered around in the kitchen broiling a couple of steaks which we could have bought at any restaurant in town. You took me in and sat me by the fireplace and opened a bottle of champagne. Then the damned phone rang and you threw me out. The very least I expected after that was an apology but I didn't even get a birthday card."

"Honey, I didn't even know it was your birthday."

"I wasn't there long enough for you to ask me."

"I'd send you some flowers but I'll be there by the time they'd get there."

"Where are you?"

"Mexico City."

"And how are the Mexican girls?"

"They couldn't compare with you."

"And as soon as you put the phone down you'll turn round and say, 'these American girls can't compare with you, *señorita!*'"

"Would I do that to you, Natalie?"

"If I gave you a chance, you would. You'd better get your ass back here to Washington."

"I've got just one more loose end to tie up and then I'm on my way."

"I hope that loose end isn't on some *señorita*. What are you doing down there anyway?"

"We're not going to talk about my job, remember?"

"I'm sure we can talk about plenty of other things if you get here."

"Two days at the outside. I promise. And which birthday was it?"

"Go to hell."

I put the phone down and went in search of the inspector. He was sitting at his desk with a pile of papers in front of him. "Did you get all the paperwork on the arrests completed yet?"

"Yes, *señor*. Now it is in the hands of the public prosecutor."

"Did you pick up Tina Rodriguez and Curtis McBride?"

"They were waiting for us. My officers arrived there and brought them in and her lawyer met them here."

"Can I talk to her?"

"She's not here. As I say they were met here by her lawyer who already had a writ of *habeas corpus* which left me no choice but to charge them both with dealing in contraband gold. The lawyer made a couple of phone calls and they got a judge down here to listen to the charges and set bail. They're both out on bail now."

"No matter. I know where they are."

SIXTEEN

I went out to a hardware store and bought myself a knife. The knife displays in Mexico would make any juvenile delinquent's heart boogie for joy. They had flick knifes, switchblades and throwing knives. I selected a ten-inch stiletto approximately Hugo's size and had them hone the edges to a razor keen edge. There was a soft leather sheath that came with it. I had been used to carrying Hugo in a special quick-release sheath on the inside of my right forearm, but without the quick-release mechanism I had to buy a couple of straps and fasten it to my left arm haft down where I could reach it with my right fingers.

Winters was tying up the phone with calls to his superior at the Treasury Department and neither he nor the inspector had any further need for me so I hitched a ride in a squad car to the airport and rented a car. I was intending to pay a visit to Tina's villa but I needed the cover of darkness to do that, so I found myself a good restaurant and gave myself a New York steak and a small bottle of wine. There is nothing like fortifying yourself before a spot of breaking and entering.

Tina and McBride had been expecting the arresting officers and it was impossible to think that they wouldn't be expecting me. She had completely disabled me and then turned me over to the consciouseless Jaime Vasquez. She must have heard reports of my escape from Vasquez's headquarters even if she had not heard of the aborted assassination attempts on President Martinez, so she must have known that I was free. There was no reason at all for her not to think that I would come looking for her. She had drugged me, kidnapped me and done her damnedest to kill me off. If she had any sense at all that villa would be guarded like Fort Knox, although I suspected that Tina would hold her life more valuable than gold.

The only way to storm such a fortress was with a team of commandos fully armed. I was going to try it on my own with nothing but an unfamiliar stiletto. I did not want any gunfire which would bring the police rushing to the scene. She had been arrested, booked and was out on bail and according to Mexican law she was innocent until proved guilty in a court of law. Even if she was found guilty of the crime as charged, the punishment for dealing in contraband gold was a very slight one. She would probably be fined several million *pesos* and put on a couple of years' probation. What we had to settle was strictly between Tina and me. I was counting on my knowledge of the villa to enable me to find access to the house.

I waited until the early hours of the morning when

any guards would be at their least alert. Then I drove to the general neighborhood and parked half a mile from the house. There was a high stone wall all the way around the house broken in three places by wrought-iron gates, two for the tenants and visitors, giving access to the garages, and one for the service entrance. The gates were of the same height as the wall but they offered more hand and footholds than the stone walls. The villa was set in about an acre of carefully landscaped park setting of trees, shrubbery, walkways and flower gardens.

I picked the service entrance and after inspecting the gate for alarm systems climbed over and dropped to the gravel surface of the driveway. I immediately moved over to the grass to deaden the sounds of my footsteps and as I moved forward I heard a muffled alarm bell. Throwing caution to the wind, I raced forward and threw myself down into the only cover I could see. I should have known that Tina was too smart to put an alarm system on the gate where everybody could see it. The place must have been trip-wired all the way round the outskirts. I looked around and I had dived into the vegetable garden, not as low as a bank of shrubbery, but I have done enough belly-crawling in Vietnam to be able to make use of whatever cover that presents itself. I wormed my down into the ground and the plants surrounded me, and found myself in the middle of a carrot patch.

It was only a few seconds before I heard the sound of passing feet and two men walked between me and the moon.

"I told Curtis he should have wired the wall with a

single strand instead of using a trip-wire."

"Damnedest thing I've ever seen. Probably some bloody cat."

They switched a couple of flashlights on and continued on round the perimeter. Forcing down the desire to nibble a carrot, I waited them out until they had had sufficient time to give me a clear run for it and then scrambled for my next cover, the base of a birch tree, standing ghostly white in the moonlight. I stood behind the tree and without being able to see the source of the voices I heard Tina say, "I don't care what you think. It's probably Carter. Do whatever you have to to keep him out of the house. Call Carlos out to do his stuff."

I heard a door slam and I risked a look around the tree. There was a figure standing on the porch, but I couldn't see who it was. He was apparently waiting for somebody because very shortly I heard more voices and from my hiding place I could see four men standing on the porch. In the still night air I could hear their voice clearly. "We have rehearsed this many times, which is why I insisted on trip-wire alarms. It might be bloody and messy but we can always bury the remains and it will not attract attention like land mines or gunfire."

I found this a fascinating point of view since I was the intended victim so I looked round the tree. I saw one man on the porch who was apparently the man Tina had been talking to and the other three men had walked down to the grounds and what I saw didn't frighten me in the least, but I did have a certain amount of respect for the man who had dreamed it up. I should have known it would have had a South American flavor to it.

The main character stood well away from the house

swinging a bolas, a long line with a ball at each end. As I watched he let go it and the bolas flew straight at a tree some thirty yards from me and entwined itself at about chest height. Once the balls had settled the other two men went into action; one prodding at bushes large enough to give a man cover with what appeared to be a pole about ten feet long with a blade at the end of it, the other sweeping a scythe across small bushes and flower beds.

Within two minutes they had completely cleared an area about thirty feet in diameter around the base of the tree of everything from the ground up to chest height. They then went on to the next tree which was the next in line from me and repeated the process. This time the guards stood back and shone flashlights up into the foliage of the tree while the bolas-twirler did his stuff. I had to admit that although the system was archaic it was effective. The tree that had hid me was too smooth for me to climb, and anyway there was not enough foliage to hide me any further up. They moved over to my tree and I got ready to move. I didn't know where the hell I was going but I had no desire to get my brains beaten out by a bolas ball, to be prodded by a ten-foot bayonet or to be scythed to death.

I let the two groundsmen move their flashlights over the foliage, then I jumped out and ran back the way I had come. I did not bother to zigzag as I would have done if somebody were shooting at me, and that was almost my undoing. I heard a whistling noise behind me and as soon as I realized that it was the bolas I fell face down on the lawn. The bolas passed harmlessly over me and wound itself around some shrubbery while I got to my feet and continued my run. I was almost at the service drive gate with no sign of cover, with two men, one carrying a scythe and the other a ten-foot bayonet, close behind me. I did the best thing I could under the circumstances and dived back into the carrot patch.

Peering between the leaves of a neighboring potato plant I saw the bolas thrower retrieve his bolas, and then the other two were on me. They hesitated and I realized that the moonlight was not reflected back from me. A pair of flashlights covered the vegetable garden and then the one with the bayonet backed off to let his scythe-bearing comrade have all the glory. A scythe is about ten feet long and I was extremely reluctant to engage in a knife battle on his terms so I slid my new stiletto out of my sleeve and then found myself a chunk of good solid earth for a distraction.

He came forward swinging the scythe and denuding the earth. From the vigor he was putting into his task I assumed that he didn't like vegetable soup. When he started on the potato patch about five or six feet from me, I lobbed the clod of earth over his head and leaped to my feet.

The results were totally unexpected. In the moonlight I saw the one who had retrieved his bolas from the shrubbery start toward the bush where the piece of earth had landed, he was followed by the man with the bayonet. The only man who was not distracted was the man whose attention I had tried to claim. As I jumped to my feet, we stood there face to face, me with a ten-inch stiletto and him with a ten-foot scythe. I lunged for him and plunged the knife into his chest, grabbed the scythe as it fell and looked at the others.

One of them was immerging his bayonet into the bush while the other stood back waiting for a shot with his bolas. Individualism is fine, but there are times when impersonation does more for you. I was wearing denim pants and jacket and in those clothes I could have easily been mistaken for the scythe wielder, so I bent down and picked up his flashlight and went back to cutting down the vegetable garden until I heard a shout summoning me to the next tree.

I had seen enough of their operation to be able to play the part and I went into the act with a great deal of enthusiasm. I did such a good job that I raised a blister on my finger. In twenty minutes we had made a complete circuit of the house and my friend the bayonet wielder and myself stood at the bottom of the steps, me with my face averted from the moonlight while Carlos climbed the steps to report to Willie Chan.

There was a short discussion while Carlos recounted how we had disturbed an intruder who had outrun us near the vegetable garden. Every tree and bush had been thoroughly searched, he told Willie. Willie tapped his teeth with his thumbnail. "If it was Carter he wouldn't have given up that easily. It was probably a burglar and we scared him off." I was quite content to accept his explanation, but by the same token I accepted the thoroughness with which the grounds had been searched. We were dismissed and while Carlos made his way to his sleeping quarters, my comrade and myself went to a small tool shed where we put our tools away for the night.

I propped the scythe in one corner and as I left the moonlight caught me across the face. He started to say something, but my clenched fist caught him on the side of the jaw before he could finish. I found some twine in the tool shed and bound his hands and feet. With him out of the way I had the grounds to myself.

Now that Willie had gone inside to report the false alarm the house had taken on an air of stillness. No lights could be seen. It was that time of day when the hangers-on had normally closed the bars and had gone to bed to work on their hangovers and before the household staff had risen to take on their duties and before the early morning fragrance of freshly perked coffee filled the air and even the crickets were asleep. I stole up the front steps, and then ignoring the main doors as the most obvious place, with my new stiletto in my hand I started to look for a window that would give me a minimum amount of trouble. There were a couple of old-fashioned swing seats on the veranda and as I passed them a voice said, "I knew you'd be back." It was Al's voice.

I turned and he had just risen from one of the swing seats. A blanket had been pushed aside and he stood there with a revolver in his hand.

"I was hoping it would be you," I said. "The last time I saw you, you had a hypodermic in your hand and were filling me full of a sleeping drug. Al, believe me, I've been looking forward to this for a long time." As I spoke I flicked the stiletto at him. It struck him in the throat and the moonlight caught the astonished look on his face. He would have liked to say something but all he could come up with was a gurgle that quickly faded into a death rattle. I stepped over to his body, took my stiletto and wiped it on his shirt.

Al had been sitting under an unlocked window which surely hadn't done the people he was supposed to be guarding one hell of a lot of good. I quickly pried the window latch back with the point of the stiletto. The thought crossed my mind to write to the manufacturer of the stiletto with one of those "unsolicited" letters that they use in advertising their wares. Two men killed and a window forced open the first time it had left its sheath. I decided against it as laying myself open to a charge of contributing to the delinquency of minors.

I bundled Al back on the swing seat again and covered him with the blanket, then pushed the window open and climbed through. The villa was built on a side of a hill and the main entrance was on the lower level and led to nothing but a staircase with beautifully balustrades leading up to the upper floors. I knew the layout of the whole place, dining room, living room and library were on the second floor and the bedrooms and bathrooms on the next floor. After all the excitement of the day, with being arrested, indicted, confronted by a judge and bailed out, I doubted very much whether Tina had gone to bed. If I knew her, and I thought I did, she would be planning some method of regaining her status: I expected to find her in the library with Curtis McBride and perhaps her criminal lawyer. Confirming that idea I could hear the sound of muted voices.

I knew the layout of the library but I was not close enough to identify the location of the voices. I rejected the idea of entering the library from the door to the passage until I had a better idea of who was sitting where. It would give me a much greater advantage to burst in from the dining room once I knew where everybody was sitting. I opened the door to the dining room and saw that the French windows leading out to the small balcony were open. Not a very surprising fact considering that the balcony was at least twenty feet up from the ground at that point.

I didn't remember any wind when I had been performing my scything chores, but the rich red drapes that covered the windows were moving. There was only one reason for that and I trod noiselessly over the plush carpet to the windows and jerked the curtains aside to reveal Willie Chan.

He was clutching a small revolver and I didn't waste any words asking what he was going to do with it. I grabbed his right wrist and exerted pressure on the nerve point, judged my distance and struck out at the base of his neck with the edge of my hand with a karate chop that would leave him unconscious for at least two or three hours. Laying him down quietly, I pressed my ear to the library door with Willie Chan's revolver in my hand.

I reached for the door handle, opened the door and strolled through as though I were a permanent guest there. Tina was sitting behind her desk in the middle of the room. Curtis McBride sat facing her with his back to the wall on my right.

"Nick, we were just talking about you," Tina exclaimed.

"I doubt if you said anything very good," I said. "My name seems to have been on everybody's lips for some time. Like Willie Chan who was about to say something mean when I clobbered him and took his gun away from his, and, poor, dear Al who was trying desperately to say something when I stuck a knife in his throat downstairs. And like Jaime Vasquez who would have liked to call me a son of a bitch but the Pacific Ocean got in his way."

"Who's Jaime Vasque'?" asked Curtis McBride.

"Curtis," I told him, "I am very glad to hear you ask that. You knew that Tina had been dealing in contraband gold, but you didn't know where it came from."

"It was the product of her secret gold mine."

"Is that what she told you? It was a treasure trove that had been buried by some escaping Nazis after World War II high up in the Andes in Peru. It was discovered by one Jaime Vasquez who tried the life of luxury but found it lacking in what he really craved, power. In exchange for a position of power in Tina's new government in Peru, he formed a band of revolutionaries dedicated to overthrowing the present government in Peru and putting Tina into power as President.

"You probably know that Tina is *persona non grata* in Peru, yet the presidency of that country is her greatest ambition. Did you ever wonder why in all her travels she would never go back to her homeland? It's because she tried to overthrow the government once before to try to replace President Martinez. If she ever shows her face in Peru again she was to have been tried for treason."

McBride said, "I knew she was involved in politics,

but I thought it was only making contributions to some political party, and trying to pull strings to make it easier for her business interests."

I said, "You keep right on thinking that and she would have had you going down the drain with her. But there's a way out for you."

He said, "I'm not a revolutionary, I'm a businessman. I don't want to get involved in all this. I'm a Canadian."

"You can get out of it very easily. I'm going to clobber you and when you wake up, you go down to police headquarters and ask them to put you in jail for protective custody. The day before yesterday our friend here had another two tries at assassinating President Martinez and there might be a few of his friends who might be a bit rough on you because of your relationship with Tina."

"Is that right?"

Tina didn't say anything but the look on her face was enough. I walked over to him and as he stood up I clipped him under the jaw with a right. It was one of my better punches and he fell back into the chair again. Tina got up from behind her desk and started to walk toward me.

"Now it's just you and me, Nick."

"No, it's just you and the population of Peru, Tina. They have a popular leader and they have not time for any misfit who would try to assassinate him."

"Is that what you came back for, Nick? To see me squirm?"

"If I wanted to see you squirm I would come to your execution."

"Why did you come back?"

"Because the job isn't finished yet."

"You took care of the gold smuggling business. Isn't that enough? Why mess with the politics of a strange country?"

"I'm not messing with politics. I got sucked into a political action that I wasn't interested in to feed your vanity and put the blame on the good old U.S.A. When will you people learn that if you come to us begging you won't get turned away? But that's not good enough for the likes of you. You wanted to assassinate President Martinez and overthrow the government and take his place. If you had succeeded, our foreign aid policy would have taken care of you. There was no need to blame it on us. Every time one of you egotistical, narcissistic chauvinists dream up some scheme of unlimited power you have to have someone to blame it on. Probably because you have not confidence in your grandiloquent plans, and before you start you must have a last line of defense for when you run out of excuses."

"Nick, why are we arguing?"

"We're not arguing. I'm just telling you where you stand."

"You came back to kill me be because I tried to have you killed."

"I didn't come here to kill you, Tina. I have no intention of killing you. I came to take you back to Peru to stand trial for treason and attempted assassination."

"It would be easier for you to kill me."

"I know it would which is why I won't do it. If you go on trial for treason, whether or not they decide to execute you it will teach you humility; something you have never had."

"There is another alternative."

"Not to my mind."

She came across to me and wound her arms round my neck and kissed me. "Nick, we had a pretty good relationship going there. Why can't we go back to it. I've got more money than we could ever spend."

"That's not the answer, Tina, and you know it. You have this lust for power and an egotistical attitude. You could never trample me underfoot, and you know it as well as I do. I have to take you back, because that is the only way you will see what true humility is."

She nibbled at my earlobe. "Nick, I love you so much, and I'll teach you to love me. We'll be a great combination."

"You have to go back to Peru, Tina."

"Can't I even pack a bag?"

Somebody can send you whatever you want, although you won't need much in a condemned cell."

"You're quite determined aren't you?"

"Just as determined as you were to kill *El Presidente*."

"Do me just one last favor. Let's have a farewell drink before we leave.

I said, "I think that's fair."

She moved away from me and walked to the bar. She put two highball glasses on the bar, a bottle of Scotch and a bottle of soda and a tray of ice cubes. She put a couple of ice cubes in each glass and poured Scotch in each, then splashed a little soda in. She came round to the front of the bar and handed me a glass.

I took it from her, poured the liquid down the sink and tipped the ice cubes into her glass, then I went behind the bar, took a fresh glass and poured a very little Scotch into it and sipped at it. Tina lifted her glass and swigged at it, then tilted it again and crunched the ice cubes and set the glass down. Again she put her arms around my neck. "Nick, kiss me. Give me a kiss that I'll remember for the rest of my life."

I put my arms around her and kissed her. I was still holding her when she died.

SEVENTEEN

When I walked off my flight in Washington, D.C., they were paging me for a message. I got got to a courtesy phone and heard an impersonal voice telling me that there was a top priority message waiting for me from the *U.S. Abraham Lincoln* somewhere in the Pacific Ocean. I got my notebook out and copied the message down verbatim and went into the lounge to decode it.

When I finished I learned that Willie Chan had been charged with Al's murder, and that Curtis McBride and Tina Rodriguez had had an argument about her political affiliations. Tina had been so upset that her clandestine activities had been discovered that she had committed suicide. Curtis McBride had asked for protective custody to defend him against attacks from revolutionaries, and that President Martinez of Peru was going to take a pleasure cruise in the Caribbean before returning to Lima to start campaigning for the next election. I tore the page out, shredded it and flushed it down the toilet and went outside to find a cab.

As usual it was raining, but the cab driver confided to me that according to his arthritis it would stop that night. On the basis of that good news I tipped him heavily outside my apartment door. I had no bag and was looking forward to a shave and a shower and a change of clothing. When I stepped through the door I stumbled over a pair of high heeled patent leather pumps. Over the bathroom doorknob was a black lace bra and in the cabinet where I normally keep my razor I found a pair of black lace panties.

It was a very quick shave and shower.